EYES OF GLASS

BENEATH THE SURFACE LIE YOUR GREATEST FEARS

GEMMA METCALFE & JOE CAWLEY

SB
SPELLBOUND
BOOKS

First Published by SpellBound Books 2023

For Mum, who birthed a weirdo and never tried to alter the fact.
This one is for you ;)
Gemma

For my trinity of saviours - Joy, David and Gemma.
You brought me back.
Joe

Prologue

Dee Warren gazes at the white-speckled expanse of grey ocean, its flatness a liquid mirror reflecting the New England sky. She purses dry lips, a frisson of fear burrowing deeper into her chest.

How easy it would be to jump.

It had all been so different in the beginning, a rags-to riches fairy tale, this very sea a pumpkin coach whisking her off to a magical land. Cinderella had betrothed her very own Prince Charming, and Bibbity, Bobbity Boo, he'd made damn sure the glass slipper fit. Who cared if it ripped her feet to shreds.

'Whatcha thinking, Momma?'

Dee jumps at the sound of Chloe's breathy voice in her ear. She feigns a smile and pulls the fourteen-year-old into a sidewards embrace, watching as the wind whips her daughter's long blonde hair into a frenzy of dancing strands. 'I was thinking of a famous quote by Gandhi,' she says. 'That humanity is like an ocean; even if a few drops are dirty, the ocean doesn't become dirty. Or something to that effect.' She studies her daughter's face for a reaction but there doesn't appear to be one. Dee has never been privy to Chloe's internal world. Not since the day she was born.

'You think too much mom,' says Chloe, rolling her eyes in that way teenagers do. Chloe gestures towards a tall figure at the edge of the cliff who points across to the horizon. 'He told me to come and fetch you.'

Dee glances over her shoulder and forces a smile. Instinctively she slips a hand into the pocket of her windcheater and grips the bottle neck.

'... so in its day, it was a magnificent achievement,' says Bill as Dee and Chloe catch up with him, as though there hasn't just been a ten-minute lull in conversation. He puts an arm around Chloe and pulls her in close, leaving Dee on the sidelines.

'A hundred and twenty years ago, Marconi sat in that tower behind us and received the first transatlantic radio transmission from a cottage in Cornwall, England,' continues Bill. 'Think about it. Before the Internet, before mobile phones... it was the first time somebody had communicated with someone else on the other side of the ocean. It was the beginning of a whole new world.'

Dee can see that he expects her to be wowed, that he needs her to mirror his wonderment. 'It's really something,' she manages. 'Just wonderful.'

Irritation flares in Bill's face but thankfully he's quick to suppress it. 'Come, we should eat. It's getting late.'

'Yes, I'm ravenous,' says Chloe eagerly.

'You two go on,' says Dee, wishing Bill would vanish right off the edge of the cliff.

Bill eyes her as though she's a flight risk.

'Mom?' Chloe frowns at her mother. 'You alright?'

'I'm fine,' she reassures them both, and realises in that moment that her words hold truth; that no matter how hard life is right now, or how small the fire of hope for a better future burns, she will never allow it to be extinguished. Not while she's a mother to this precious girl. 'I'd like a moment to myself. That's all.'

Dee waits until Bill and Chloe are some distance away before removing the bottle from her coat pocket and launching it out to sea. It spins through the air, glistening with sparks of sunlight as the pale orb slowly slips behind the rows of colourful townhouses dotting St John's harbour behind them.

Who will read my words? Dee wonders, her eyes now fixed on the horizon.

Who will know my truth.

Chapter One
Lyra

6 months later

I FLING OPEN THE BEDROOM WINDOW AND HURL THE car keys down at my cheating rat of a boyfriend. 'Seriously Tom, just leave before I lose it!'

'You're being irrational. Let me back in.' Tom scurries across the front lawn and bends over to retrieve the keys, giving Karen at number ten a bird's-eye view of his pasty white backside.

'Irrational! Are you serious? I've just caught you dry humping your secretary, in our bed! I mean honestly, can you be anymore cliché!'

'And I'm truly sorry for that,' pleads Tom, balling his hands into fists and hammering the front door. 'Please Lyra, you were never meant to find out like this.'

'Oh, apologies. That makes it all alright then.'

Okay, so Tom has a point, of sorts. Technically, I wasn't meant to be home from the writer's retreat until this afternoon. If it wasn't for the warning about the North Atlantic Current and the Gulf Stream ganging together and threatening to mug everybody in Galway Bay with arse-kicking winds, I'd still be discussing the finer points of prose with my fellow wordsmiths, blissfully unaware that my boyfriend was balls deep in Fifty Shades of Adultery!

'It's been eating away at me. I haven't slept for weeks!'

'Oh, my heart bleeds! Come inside and let me fix you a Horlicks!'

It's so obvious now, of course it is - late nights, new aftershave, not to mention a sudden love of Adele. I mean *Adele,* for Christ's sake! Well, if he doesn't remove himself from the lawn soon, he'll *feel* something, and sure as shit it won't be my love!

'Lyra, my underpants, I'm begging you.' Tom is now concealing his manhood with a garden gnome.

'I wouldn't have bothered with that. A peg would have done the trick.'

'Jesus, you're brutal, you know that?' He sighs dramatically. 'Well, if you won't let me in, then just throw me down some clothes. 'Being naked in public is a criminal offence,' he stage whispers. 'Do you want me to end up in the clinker?'

'Only you're not naked, are you? You're wearing socks. Christ, you actually kept your socks on!'

Marching over to the chest of drawers, I swipe out a handful of boxers. As much as I want to see Tom freeze his nuts off, I can't risk the Nichols, our elderly neighbours, having heart attacks. Mr. Nichols only had a bypass last month and Mrs. Nichols has forever been at the mercy of her nerves. The sight of Tom's flaccid penis on a wet Monday morning could quite literally spell the end for both of them.

'Here!' I toss the underwear out of the window. 'Let's see if your tart still wants you after *she's* scrubbed your gussets for a week!'

Plucking the pair of threadbare Calvin's from the hanging basket, Tom hops around on one leg as he attempts to reclaim his modesty.

I pull out a dusty holdall from underneath the bed and stuff in

Tom's clothes. I should have known by our wardrobe space alone that we were doomed; his side is all neat and colour-coded, and then there's mine, a crumpled mess of black. We're too different, Tom and I, always have been. He enjoys people, parties and an easy life. And me? Mrs 'alternative,' a self-proclaimed Emo who would rather be lost in lyrics and books than engage in real life, with real people - Tom included. Can I blame him really?

My tear ducts sting, but I know I won't cry.

I haven't cried in thirty years and I'm not about to start now.

'Fecking eejit.'

I slam the front door, leaving Tom to pack the rest of his crap, though he's kindly informed me he'll be wanting the house back in a week or two due to it being his.

Pulling my beanie low over my head, partly due to the cold but mostly because I don't care to make eye-contact with anyone, I head for Gratton Beach, the only place on earth that has the power to relax my mind. What the hell am I going to do now?

Two years ago I did something I vowed I never would; I let my guard down, gave up my poky, yet ridiculously cheap, seafront flat for the sake of love. Now rental prices are through the roof and my career as a writer isn't exactly snowballing.

Reaching the beach, I remove my Doc Martins and inhale a lungful of sea air; usually the salty brine calms me but today even the ocean seems ominous; a chorus of squawking seagulls flash white fury across a leaden sky as frothing waves foretell of stormy times ahead.

As always when I'm here my thoughts turn to mammy. She loved Gratton Beach, often proclaiming that the ocean spray was *for sure the best medicine around*, though she often said that about me too; 'Lyra, you're my happy pill, darlin.' In the end, the sea air wasn't enough to save her. And neither was I.

I edge forward, tensing as the icy water of Galway Bay rushes over my bare feet. I'm a paddler more than a swimmer. The thought of being out of my depth, both literally and figuratively, always put paid to the idea of swimming lessons.

The truth is, I'm nothing short of a fuck-up. I managed to hide it for a while, even convinced myself that I could be normal, if only by association, as Tom's girlfriend. The cracks started to appear last year, when Tom spoke of marriage, and worse still, of starting a family.

I couldn't. I can't. Not ever.

What the hell am I going to do? I have no family, no real job, and now no home or boyfriend. Okay, so I have *some* money. My debut thriller, *Mother,* did surprisingly well, even hitting the Amazon top spot, (albeit for three hours before Angela Bloody Marsons swooped in.) But that was over a year ago. For months I've been trying to write a second book but I don't have even a seed of an idea. At best my savings will stretch to a few months in a bedsit.

Like my life, the beach is littered with crap, everyday items left behind by the selfish and lazy - plastic cups and bags, straws, broken glass. I stuff a discarded Aldi carrier bag in my pocket, then stoop to pluck a wine bottle from the gloopy sand with the intention of putting it in a recycling bin. I'm surprised at how light it feels given it's corked. Holding it up towards the sunlight, I notice that there's something inside, a piece of paper, I think. I tease out the cork and shake out the contents.

Chapter Two

Lyra

And never forget dear finder of this message,
'We are all lonely voyagers sailing on life's ebb tide.'
Shannon L. Alder

Yours Truthfully,
Dee Warren
8 Tuthill Ln #27, Edgartown, MA 02539
United States
Tel: +1 508 627- 3202

Jeez. Could this be genuine? An actual transatlantic message. It's dated 1st January 2022, so six months ago. Not exactly historic, but I'm gobsmacked, nonetheless.

The note also appears to contain a poem, though a combination of not wearing my specs and the arse kicking wind makes it difficult to read. Clutching the note in one hand and the bottle in the other, I head for home where I can read it properly, though the word 'home,' is quickly followed by the sickening realisation that I know longer have one.

It's strangely eerie walking into an empty house, ridiculous really as Tom and I were forever passing ships in the night; him working all day as a recruitment manager (recruiting notches on his bedpost, so it seems), and me rising at noon and working late into the night; though when I say working, I mean scrolling through Instagram while singlehandedly keeping Ben & Jerry's in business.

Not bothering to remove my coat, I place the bottle down on the coffee table, grab my specs and collapse onto the couch.

'What the...' I re-read the letter, slower this time, and then a third time. As I thought, it's a poem, which in itself is bizarre. I would have assumed a message found in a bottle would be a time capsule, mentioning current affairs and the author's life. This poem is about the bottle's journey across The Atlantic, or at least on the surface it is. I'm sure there's some clever subtext going on, but poetry never was my strongpoint.

I contemplate calling the phone number, but what will I say? 'Oh hi, I'm Lyra, I found your bottle in Galway, Ireland.' Then what? A stilted conversation because neither of us quite knows telephone etiquette for bottle discovery. I can imagine it now; 'Jeepers, that's swell Lyra. Y'all having a nice day?'

'Oh you know how it is Dee, this morning I walked in on my boyfriend screwing a titty blonde with an outrageous sex face. How about you?'

'Gee, that sounds grim. I'm making blueberry pancakes.'

Oh, sod it. What's the worst that can happen? Fishing my

mobile from my coat pocket, I quickly tap in the number before I have a chance to bottle it (pardon the pun). Lord, even the ring-tone is an all-American-howdy-partner fanfare rather than a hurry-up-and-answer whine.

'Hello?'

A girl's voice, surely? I stifle a nervous laugh. 'Oh, how you doing? I'm Lyra.' The next few seconds are a blur as I garble on about Ireland and the bottle and how I hate littering, but well, in this exception and... *Jesus, shut up Lyra.*

'You mentioned a poem from mom? In a bottle.' The girl's voice rises several octaves and not just in that way Americans do naturally. 'Oh my God, I'm psyched!'

'Yeah, me too.' I realise I sound winded, so pause to take a breath. 'So, I'd love to chat to her, your mammy.'

I feel the shift in atmosphere before I hear it in the girl's reply. I glance down at the poem, every word now making sense. 'Say that again?'

'She died,' repeats the girl, her voice now breaking. 'Six months ago. She killed herself.'

Chapter Three
Lyra

The line falls silent. 'Hello...' I realise I don't even know the poor girl's name. 'Hello. You still there?'

A soft snivel is followed by a sad little laugh. 'Yes I'm here. The mention of mom, you know, it's thrown me a little.'

You're not the only one is what I want to say, but thankfully I keep my social awkwardness under control. I ought to offer some sort of condolence or suggest I call back once she's processed the news, yet all I manage is a non-committal 'umm.'

'I'm Chloe, by the way. Chloe Deanna Warren,' says the girl; her voice high-pitched and excitable which seems odd given the bombshell she's just dropped from a great fecking height. 'Deanna after mom,' she continues with the same enthusiasm. 'Though everyone just called her Dee, though I prefer Deanna because it sounds more classical, don't you think?'

'It's lovely.' I scratch around in my head for something useful to add.

'Did you say your name was Laura?' asks Chloe, saving me from blathering on about time being a healer.

'Lyra,' I correct. 'Though you'd be surprised how many times I've been called Laura in my...'

'And you said you live in Ireland?' Chloe interrupts, her voice now so high it sounds laced with helium.

'Yes. Galway. And you live in Massachusetts?'

'Chappaquiddick,' replies Chloe with a swell of pride. 'Chappy they call it. It's an island... pretty famous, mostly because Teddy Kennedy had that car accident here and killed a girl.'

I vaguely recall watching a film about the incident. If I remember rightly the accident was the catalyst for Kennedy not running for president. 'Look Chloe, I just wanted to say I really am sorry to hear about your mammy,' I manage at last. 'I lost mine too. So, I get it, you know, how hard it can be.'

Chloe sighs. 'Nobody on Chappy gets it. Well maybe Jackson, he's my older stepbrother and he doesn't have a mom either because she left when he was small and he's never seen her since, but it's not really the same is it?'

'I guess not.'

'Besides, he's a real pain. So immature, honestly.'

'And how old are you, Chloe?'

'Fifteen last month.'

I'm surprised. She sounds a lot younger.

'Bill threw me an awesome party,' she continues without taking a breath. 'I had a black limousine, a red carpet... oh and a live band, like the coolest.'

I stifle a yawn, then suddenly it dawns on me! 'God, I'm so sorry, I've just realised it must be the middle of the night where you are. I didn't think.'

'Ah it's cool. It's just gone five, but I don't sleep much anyhow, and Bill will be up soon. He works so hard, he's an inspiration, and Jackson won't even be home yet. He's a night owl.'

'Right.' I feel as though I need a lie down myself after talking to Chloe, or rather listening to Chloe. 'I noticed you said Bill, so he isn't your daddy then?'

Chloe scoffs. 'Daddy, that's funny. No, Bill isn't my father, he married my mom three years ago. The wedding was awesome. Like out of this world!'

'So would you like me to post you the note?' I wince as I realise how offhand I sound. 'Sorry, that came out wrong. I'm not trying to get rid of you or anything.'

'Will you call me again?' asks Chloe, her voice quieter now, as if unsure of herself.

'Of course, I'd love to.'

'Thank you,' she says, which makes my heart sink further. 'I like you Lyra, I feel we connect.

'I like you too Chloe,' I say, wondering why she isn't asking me to read her the note. Though I guess her mammy's death is still so raw.

'Okay, well call back tomorrow okay, same time, bye now.'

The line goes dead.

For a moment I don't move. What the bejesus has just happened?

I read Dee's poem again, my insides somersaulting as I realise what it is.

Chapter Four

January 1st, 2022

The lonely bottle whispers far,
Echoing across the brine,
Dreaming of breaking free, a star,
From depths where currents twine.
Lunar tides have left it dull,
Once a gleaming sight,
Now battered, misused, and null,
Crushed in the ocean's might.
Purposeless it drifts and spins,
With vacant glassy eyes,
Though willed by waves and winds,
Its shattered pieces rise.
If by chance you chance upon
This bottle worn and torn,
Gather each fragment, one by one,

And hear its tale forlorn.
The remnants of its glassy shell,
Hold truths of the deep,
A prayer to you who finds it well,
To help the ones who weep.
So if you read these words today,
Harken to the bottle's plea,
Take it gently, don't delay,
And set its spirit free.

And never forget dear finder of this message,

"We are all lonely voyagers sailing on life's ebb tide."

Shannon L. Alder

Yours truthfully,
Dee Warren
8 Tuthill Ln #27, Edgartown, MA 02539
United States
Tel: +1 508 627- 3202

Chapter Five

Lyra

'I've written a new poem,' announces Chloe the second the line connects. 'Do you want to hear it?'

It's now been two weeks since I found what I believe is her mother's suicide note and we've spoken daily. Or rather Chloe has spoken daily and I've listened.

'Of course. I love your poetry.'

'Amazing! Thank you. It's still pretty rough so don't judge me too harshly, okay?' Chloe laughs in that sweet, childish way I've become accustomed to.

In truth, I look forward to our chats just as much as she does. It's somewhat of an enigma as normally I can't tolerate people for long periods, unless of course they're fictional; Atticus Finch, now there's somebody I wouldn't mind squandering my transatlantic minutes on.

'Come off it, Chloe, you write beautifully. Anyway, you know you're much better at poetry than I am.' I take a sip of now freezing-cold coffee as I wait for her to begin. It isn't lost on me how she still hasn't asked to hear her mother's poem, though I'm relieved because it's likely to traumatise the poor kid.

'So, it's called *Reflection*,' Chloe begins, clearing her throat.

'Though that might just be a working title... I don't know... anyway... okay... here goes. I gaze into the mirror, though it isn't me I see. A single tear slips down my cheek, how can this be?' She stops dead. 'It's so bad isn't it, tell me if it's really bad, Lyra.'

'No of course not.' In truth, Chloe's poetry makes me feel inept. If only I could write so honestly. Perhaps that's where I'm going wrong. Stephen King is famously quoted as saying, 'Fiction is the truth inside the lie.' *Mother*, for sure, was my heart bled dry, the words darker than ink. Now I'm unsure if I have anything left to give.

'Lyra, you still there?'

'Sorry, carry on,' I urge.

Chloe swallows loudly. 'The stranger staring back, is broken up inside, shattered like glass, desperate to hide. Her eyes bleed sorrow, from the pain of rejection. She's out of reach now, trapped in my reflection.'

I sit open-mouthed, my heart aching for her. 'Shit. That's deep.'

'But... did... you... like... it?' she says with trepidation.

'Well of course, but...' What do I even say? *Good use of simile.* 'I mean it's really good Chloe but... well, is it a reflection of how you see yourself?'

'Ha! Love the pun there. You're a smart one, Lyra.'

I don't admit it wasn't intentional. 'Chloe seriously, that's pretty full-on. Are you sure you're okay?'

For Christ's sake Lyra, of course she isn't okay! Her mammy's topped herself and she's writing poetry about bleeding sorrow. God, I'm out of my depth here. I can barely manage my own screwed up head without poking around in some hormonal teenager's on the other side of the Atlantic.

'It's just a poem, Lyra,' retorts Chloe, huffing. 'Don't be like Marie. She's always trying to turn my words back at me like I'm some sort of crazy weirdo. She tried to get me to see a shrink you know.'

'Who's Marie?' I ask, not recalling her ever being mentioned.

'Our housekeeper. Likes to stick her nose in all the time. Anyway, listen…' Chloe's voice shoots up an octave. 'My stepdad Bill is here and he wants to speak to you. I've told him there's no need, you're not a lunatic or anything but he's just being protective, I guess.'

'Okay, sure. I guess that makes sense.' Panic sits beneath my calm exterior. What in God's name am I going to say to Bill? Oh Jesus, what kind of hole have I gone and gotten myself…

'Hello, this is Bill Warren.'

'Hello, Bill, nice to meet you. Chloe's right, I'm not a nutter or anything, well at least my psychiatrist doesn't say so.' I emit a strange, high-pitched laugh.

'Okay,' replies Bill, deadpan. He's well-spoken, his voice deep, oozing authority. 'You found a bottle belonging to my late wife, I believe?'

'I did, here in Ireland. Galway to be exact.'

'That's good.'

'Yeah, it's lush.' Silence hangs on the line. 'Well, I was shocked in truth, like gobsmacked,' I continue, vomiting random words. 'I mean, a message in a bottle! Never thought I'd be lucky enough to find something like that. Well, not *lucky* of course, obviously what happened to your wife was terrible… condolences by the way… but yeah, nice for me, I guess.'

Nice for me? Seriously?

'It's very kind of you to let us know,' replies Bill drily. 'On Irish shores too. Dee had Irish ancestry. It's a shame she's no longer with us to hear the good news.'

'Oh, it's no bother.' *No, bother? Shoot me now!* 'I mean, it would have been nice for Dee, an achievement.' I wince. 'Look, I really am sorry for your loss.'

'I appreciate your condolences.'

Jeez! The guy has no emotion. It's like talking to a robot. I can hear he's covered the mouthpiece with his hand and is talking to someone, probably Chloe.

Bill's voice then drops to an almost whisper. 'Lyra, listen. I need to talk with you, about something important.'

'Oh?' My heart pounds.

'As I'm sure you're aware, Chloe is dealing with a lot of emotions right now. Losing her mother, especially under the circumstances, has affected her badly.'

Shattered like glass, desperate to hide.

'Yes, I kind of got that from her.'

'She won't talk to anyone. But since speaking to you, I don't know, she seems to have come out of her shell a bit, shall we say, which is wonderful of course, and I'm in no way trying to discourage it...'

'But...' I interject.

Bill hesitates. 'She's been trying to persuade me to invite you here. She talks of little else.'

'Erm... okay.'

'I told her it was a bad idea, no offense to you, but we don't know you, and things here are still very raw.'

'I understand that... and agree, I mean, I don't know you guys either and...'

'So, you're not all that keen to come, no?' The relief in Bill's voice is palpable.

'Well, I mean it's not that I don't want to, it's just...' I briefly consider saying yes. In truth, visiting Chappaquiddick and reuniting the Warrens with the bottle would be incredible. I also have Tom breathing down my neck for the house back so a few weeks to clear my head and organise my life would be a blessing, but it's obvious that Bill doesn't want me there. 'I do have a lot of work on,' I say, begrudgingly.

'Of course, I understand. You don't really know us, plus you have too much work. Is that right?'

It dawns on me that Bill is manipulating the conversation to not come across as the bad guy. 'Excuse me a second, I'll just relay this to Chloe,' he says brightly.

Another round of inaudible mumbling is followed by the sound of Chloe wailing. I can't tell if it's genuine or just the act of a child trying to get their own way.

'Lyra? You're saying you don't want to come and visit me? Is that right?'

Chloe must have picked up another handset.

'Chloe, put the phone down, please,' says Bill calmly.

'Lyra, tell me. I thought you liked me... that we were friends. Why don't you want to see me?'

'She didn't say it like that, Lovebug...' continues Bill.

'It's not *that*, Chloe,' I reiterate. 'I'd love to see you, it's just...' I fumble around for the right words. If I explain to Chloe that it's Bill who has just made me feel about as welcome as a hole in a condom, I'll land him in trouble. I feel sorry for him; dealing with a grieving teen's tantrums can't be much fun.

'So why then?' persists Chloe. 'We have a guest house and everything. You can have time and space to write. Oh, and we've got a beach... and a pool... you'd love it here. Tell her Bill.'

'But Lyra explained that she doesn't really know us, didn't you, Lyra? It would be... awkward, Chloe... so perhaps we give it a little more time and then...'

'But you do know us?' perseveres Chloe. 'Well, you know me at least, we connect, you get me... or maybe you were just pretending.'

I hear her voice breaking. 'I'm not sure your stepfather thinks it's the best idea,' I say, the guilt too heavy a burden to carry alone. 'I'd love to come but...'

'So, if Bill says it's okay, you'll come?' Chloe is now practically shouting. 'Say she can come, Bill... please, for me.'

There's an awkward pause.

'Please,' says Chloe in a desperate tone.

Bill lets out a long breath. 'Okay, but...'

Chloe's desperation turns to excitement, like a car dealer on the verge of a sale. 'So will you come now, Lyra?' she begs. 'We'll pay for the flights, everything.'

'Well, I don't know, I...' How the hell can I say no?

'Lyra, please come,' says Bill, now seemingly resigned. 'It would mean the world to Chloe and therefore it would mean the world to me.'

'Are you sure?' I ask, feeling the first flutters of excitement.

I catch the faintest of sighs. 'I'm sure.'

Chapter Six
Bill

Bill puts the phone down and stands staring at it for a moment. Through the porch window, the leaves on the maple trees quiver in the Atlantic breeze, the only movement in what could otherwise be a revered landscape masterpiece like the Thomas Cole hanging in his study. Even the gunmetal-blue strip of Nantucket Sound at the end of the lawn is untarnished with the usual daubs of white that decorate the ocean swell. It's a sure sign that change is on the way. And change, of any kind, is something Bill Warren does his best to avoid.

He reaches for the phone again and pushes the redial button.

'You're the best.' Chloe's effervescent voice behind him makes him jump. Her hazel eyes sparkle with excitement, but Bill knows, like the Cape Cod weather, her mood can change from one extreme to the other in a flash.

He gently replaces the receiver and inhales deeply through his nose as he straightens his six-foot-four frame.

She throws her arm around his waist, her cheek pressed into his chest. She looks up at him, her face still resting on his white Brioni shirt. 'I love you, you know,' she says, those eyes now assuming sincerity. 'I'd do anything for you, you know that don't you?'

Bill strokes his thumb gently over Chloe's cheek, her skin softer than butter. 'Look, lovebug, I'm not one hundred percent that it's a good idea to invite a stranger into our home...'

'She's not a stranger, silly,' interrupts Chloe. 'She's, my friend.'

'She's a stranger to me, though. You know I'm a private person, so if she does come... and it's still an *if*... anything can happen between now and then... I don't want you spouting off about our personal lives...' he pauses, though knows it needs to be said. 'About what happened with mom... understand?'

'I promise,' says Chloe. She mimics zipping her lips and putting a key in the back pocket of her jeans.

Bill watches her bound away. 'Just for you,' she winks, patting the imaginary key.

He glances again at the phone, his jaw clenched.

Chapter Seven
Lyra

It would appear that standing out from the crowd isn't a thing in Martha's Vineyard. As I watch the small luggage carousel start to rotate, I'm aware of myriad faces staring at me; a mother holding tight her two wide-eyed children as I pass; a salesman clutching a laptop case to his chest as if I'm about to mug him; and a couple of teens immaculately dressed in beige pants and pale blue Oxford shirts. They all look at me as though I've crash-landed from another planet, which I guess is true. Let's face it, I'm intimidating at the best of times with my face piercings and goth eye makeup but after several hours holed up in a tin can, I must look positively demonic.

'Lyra? Over here!'

A Latino-looking lady in a bright yellow dress patterned with red and green watermelon slices waves frantically at me.

Bill mentioned that he would likely send his housekeeper to meet me at the airport, so I'm assuming this is her. I heave my case off the carousel and drag it towards her. 'Hey? I'm...'

'Lyra, I know. I'm Marie. How was your journey, *mi bonita*?' A smile stretches from one cluster of gold earring hoops to the other, all framed by curly, black, shoulder-length hair.

'I'm grand, thanks, the journey...' but before I've finished, Marie's got me in a bear hug and won't let go.

'You're exactly how I imagined,' she says, now cupping my face in her hands.

Wow. Not many would envisage a woman they hadn't met as having bright orange hair, wrist tattoos and Doc Martins. 'You looked me up on social media, I guess.'

'No. I'm just blessed with a gift,' she says, 'From God.' She looks up at the wooden ceiling, crosses herself and silently mouths *gracias mi Dios*. '*Vamos*, let's go.' She links my arm and we stroll out into the sunlight.

'How far is it to the house from here?' I ask, the fatigue of travelling for almost twelve hours now starting to kick in.

'Just short of half an hour, including the ferry,' says Marie as she hauls my suitcase into the front luggage space of an old Volkswagen Beetle. She tries to slam the bonnet shut but my case is too bulky. 'It'll be alright,' she says after weighing up the problem for a moment, and we climb in her car leaving it semi-open.

'You sure that's okay?' I ask.

She smiles. 'We'll see, won't we?' After a couple of false starts, the engine splutters to life. 'Don't let me down,' she says to the sky. 'I told Bill I needed to take his car but he wouldn't let me,' she says as the car lurches forward then stalls. 'Doesn't trust my driving, apparently.'

I nod and smile, pulling my safety belt as tight as it will go. It's just as well. I soon learn that Marie isn't a lover of being told what to do - especially when it comes to white lines and road signs. Thankfully the road is quiet as we weave from one side to the other and disregard any stop signs while she chats endlessly about her family, the island and the Warrens.

I try to sound interested but it's been ages since I've been out of Ireland and my eyes are torn between closing, and taking in the scenery of dense woodland, sudden patches of open fields, and lawns surrounding Little House on the Prairie-style homesteads.

It's not a million miles from the landscapes of Galway, except the houses are bigger, the clouds smaller, and judging from my first two encounters, first with Chloe and now with Marie, the people more over-enthusiastic about *everything*.

Like Chloe, Marie is a bundle of excited energy. Everybody and everything are *so* amazing or incredible, and every new proclamation of her love for somebody or something is preceded by *I promise you*; 'I promise you, it's the most beautiful place on earth'; 'I promise you, you won't meet a nicer person'; 'I promise you, you'll love it here'.

As a sign welcomes us to Edgartown, the woodland wanes and the pastel, clapperboard houses are drawn closer to the road. Then we're on Main Street with its white picket fences and American flags poking from perfect porches. The road narrows as we enter the commercial area with its neat shops selling ice cream, boating equipment, and artisan jewellery, before the commerce abruptly ends at a seafood restaurant overlooking the harbour.

'Here we are,' announces Marie cheerily. 'The famous Chappy ferry.'

Chappaquiddick Island seems close enough to swim to, almost close enough to jump.

'Five hundred and twenty-seven feet between here and the crazy people,' says Marie, staring at the stretch of water.

I glance over at her. 'Why do you say that?'

Marie jerks the car onto the three-car, flat-bed ferry. 'Say what?'

'The crazy people. You said over there are the crazy people. Why?'

A man appears at the driver's window before she can answer. 'How are you today, Marie?'

Marie hands him a ticket. 'Oh, I'm good, Clint. And you? Kids alright?'

'Couldn't be better,' he chirps and moves on to the car behind.

Marie turns and smiles. 'You'll find out.'

I want to push for more, but the ferry door suddenly clangs shut and the engine growls into life.

This is it, I think, my stomach in knots. No going back. We chug towards an offload bay flanked by twin swathes of golden sand. It feels manufactured; colour-saturated like a scene from a 60s Hollywood film.

In less than a minute we drive onto Chappaquiddick island. A warm breeze wafts through the open windows as we weave through the island's heart, a lush patchwork of oaks, beech, birch and pines. Fanned by the breeze, soothed by the hum of tyres on tarmac, and exhausted from my travels, my eyes finally concede.

'Chloe told me you found a message in a bottle,' says Marie.

My eyes open again. Christ, the bottle! How could I have forgotten? 'Yeah,' I murmur, 'it's how we met.'

'Incredible! I promise you, that's one of the most amazing stories I've ever heard.' Marie is averting her gaze from the road for longer than I deem comfortable.

I nod. 'It sure is.'

'What did it say?'

I could relay the poem now, word for word, but I'm not comfortable sharing it with the housekeeper without Bill or Chloe's permission. 'I'll find it and show you sometime.'

'Was it from Dee, God bless her soul?' persists Marie.

I nod.

Marie remains quiet for a while. 'Only there's something not quite right about that, about her... passing, shall we say.'

'What do you mean?'

Marie sighs, her eyes misting. 'She was beautiful Dee, inside and out, I promise you, but something troubles me. I'm not sure it all adds up.' She frowns, shakes her head, then suddenly brightens again. 'We're here!'

I sit up and stretch. 'Oh. My. God! You're joking.' The Warren's house is massive, like something you'd see on MTV cribs or The Fresh Prince of Bel-Air.

Marie notices my shock. 'Not bad, huh?'

'Not bad? It's bigger than my town, and I'm not exaggerating.'

The setting sun throws what seems like golden stage lighting onto the white and beige façade, illuminating a bright green backdrop of pines that frame the two-story mansion. I guess there must be at least eight bedrooms judging from the number of upstairs windows, each looking out to a strip of sand at the end of a sprawling lawn. 'Wow,' is all I can muster. I picture myself standing on the white-fenced balcony, coffee in hand, watching the waves roll in and out, or sat in a rocking chair between the pillars of the downstairs porch jotting thoughts on a notepad. Without doubt, it's the most perfect writer's retreat I could wish for – albeit a damn sight bigger than I would ever need.

Marie puts a hand on my knee. 'Ready to meet the Warrens?'

I'm nervous but hope it doesn't show. 'Let's go.'

Chapter Eight
Chloe

Chloe stands at the window, one hand drawing a net curtain across her face. The other hand covers her mouth as she gnaws at her thumbnail. Bill would kill her if he could see her now. 'Chewing is for rats,' he'd snap.

She watches Marie get out of the car. She's wearing that god-awful dress again, the one that makes her look like a trifle. *Jeez, she's so embarrassing.*

Chloe's eyes strain to see Lyra, desperate to see how she steps out of the car, how she wears her hair, her shoes, to gauge her reaction to the house, and to Chloe's world.

The bedroom door opens and the padding of bare feet on floorboards announces her stepbrother, Jackson's arrival. He stands beside her, dressed only in boxer shorts. 'She's here then,' he says.

'You stink.'

He throws her a look.

They both stand and watch in silence.

As Lyra emerges from the car, Chloe jerks back.

'Nervous?' Jackson mocks. 'Thought you were soulmates.'

'Ssshhh.'

Lyra gazes up at the house. Chloe studies the way she moves, the way she's dressed, the boldness of her make-up, how she places her hands on her hips, the nervous smile she flashes at Marie. Chloe smiles to herself. Lyra's everything she expected.

Jackson leans into her, his sour breath hot in her ear. 'I'm warning you.' He grabs her elbow and squeezes tight. 'Not a fucking word.'

Chapter Nine
Lyra

I put one hand on the Beetle's bonnet and it springs wide open. How it didn't spill my luggage is anyone's guess.

'See? Told you it'd be fine.' Marie crosses her chest for what seems like the hundredth time already. 'If he managed to get the disciples across the seas of Galilee, I'm sure keeping your bags safe was a cinch.' Her eyes crease with a smile. 'Anyway, we're the same size. You could have borrowed my clothes.'

Her frilly, fruit-imprinted dress makes me want to cross myself too.

'No, you don't, *bonita*.' She bats my hand away as I attempt to lift out the case. 'That's my job. You don't pack light, do you?' she huffs, dumping the case onto the gravelled driveway. 'Nothing valuable in there, I hope?'

'I wish. Most of my clothes are from a charity shop.' I glance down at my ripped jeans and Led Zeppelin hoodie. 'I should have packed something posher. What are they going to think if I rock up at supper like this?'

'They're just people, Lyra.' She puts a reassuring hand on my arm. 'They might have more money than us, but they're no better... or happier for that matter.'

It's the sort of thing Mammy would say, and I'd love to believe it, but how can living in a place like this not breed happiness? Everything from the sunlit lawn to the gleaming white symmetry of their enormous home is picture-perfect. Though I'm quickly reminded that Dee Warren was anything but happy.

'Oh my God! You're here!' Chloe sprints towards me, barefoot. 'I didn't sleep a wink last night!'

'Easy, girl,' says Marie. 'Don't smother the poor woman. She's just arrived.'

'I'm so happy you're actually right here in front of me,' gushes Chloe, now squeezing the crap out of me.

I manage to extricate myself, but Chloe's beaming face remains inches from mine. She's not what I envisioned; she's shorter than her Insta photos suggest, and her skin isn't quite as flawless without the filters. She's a natural beauty though. Her long blonde hair glistens with a dozen shades of gold that tumble down her white cotton crop-top and onto faded denim shorts. To me, she's the epitome of a Californian surf chick, yet here we are in Massachusetts.

'I'm sorry, I'm sorry...' Her huge, dark-brown eyes glisten with concern. 'You're happy to see me though, aren't you?'

'Of course!' My words come out all choked. Jesus Christ, what's wrong with me? Hugs and emotions all in one day! I quickly convey that it's just jetlag.

'Come on, let me show you around,' Chloe grabs my wrist and yanks me in the direction of the house. 'You're going to love it.'

'What about my suitcase?'

'Yeah, it's awesome, I love the colour.'

I glance back at Marie who rolls her eyes. 'Crazy people,' she mouths with a wry smile.

'Here we are!' Chloe drags me through the front door into a grand hallway. Elegant wall lights throw soft circles around framed paintings of what I assume are local landscapes, while white, waist-high wood panels half cover the marigold-painted walls. It has the feel of a well-curated museum, everything affected to impress visitors.

Chloe skips up three steps, urging me to follow. Those words hit me again. Oh. My. God. The living room looks like the centrefold of an interior design magazine. Pastel-blue soft furnishings mirror the colour of the ocean that glints in the distance through floor-to-ceiling glass doors. In an alcove beneath an interior balcony, eight stiff-back chairs are spaced evenly around a honey-hued dining table, which itself is set with placemats, silverware, and linen serviettes held in perfect neat rolls by ivory napkin rings. *I wonder if anybody actually eats here.* It looks too neat to disturb.

Chloe plonks herself down onto a gingham couch. 'Do you like it?' she beams.

'I'm shook as a hand at mass.'

'Huh?'

'I'm stunned, so I am. It's amazing. You're so lucky to live here.'

'I know,' she grins, though the smile doesn't quite reach her eyes.

'So, where's your stepdad?'

'Bill? He's at work, of course.' Chloe rolls her eyes. 'He'll be home for dinner. Let me fix you a drink.' Before I can catch my breath, Chloe's jumped back up and is darting across the room shouting about Coke floats.

I follow her into the kitchen. I say 'kitchen', it's the size of my whole house and has two dining areas as well as an island as big as a double bed. Chloe scoops ice cream from a huge tub of vanilla and plops a blob into two tall glasses of Coke. 'Watch them fizz,' she says, bending so her eyes are level with the frothing mass. 'Cool, huh?' She throws in a straw and slides one of the glasses towards me, leaving a trail of murky brown on the grey, marble. She hoists herself onto the worktop and watches me as I take a sip. 'Delish, isn't it?' she asks eagerly.

'Mmm,' I nod. It actually tastes of gone-off milk, but I don't want to hurt her feelings.

She slurps her drink and kicks her heels against the dishwasher, all the time running her eyes up and down me. Her behaviour is a stark reminder that she's only fifteen, a child thrown into a world of grief. I try to think of something poignant to say but to my horror, my stomach gets there first and growls loudly.

'Jeez. You must be hungry?' Chloe jumps down off the worktop and pads to the door. 'Marie!' she bellows. 'Lyra's hungry!'

'No, honestly.' I feel my cheeks burn. 'I'm okay, honestly, I...'

'Marie!' she barks again, this time with annoyance in her voice. She glances back at me and shakes her head. 'I'm sure she ignores me on purpose sometimes.'

'Chloe, I'm sure Marie has enough to do without pandering to my belly.'

'I'll fix you something,' she huffs, hands now-on-hips like a spoilt brat who's been read her Miranda rights. 'Peanut butter and jelly okay?'

'Sure,' I agree, if only to keep the peace. 'When you say jelly though, you mean jam, right?' I ask, in an attempt to lighten the mood.

Chloe frowns. 'Jam? I dunno. If jam is jelly, I guess so.' She pulls a loaf of bread, a tub of peanut butter and a single-serve jam sachet from the fridge. I notice it takes her a good few seconds of trial and error to locate the cutlery drawer. 'You were saying about being lucky... to live here, I mean,' she says, now furiously sawing at the sachet with a carving knife. 'You're right, I am lucky.' She glares at me, the knife pointing at me like a wagging finger. 'But I'm not spoilt, honestly I'm not.'

'I know,' I say, unconvincingly. 'I just felt bad you asking Marie to make me food, that's all.'

'That's what we pay her for,' she retorts, her eyebrows knitting together in confusion. 'We give her money and she does whatever we ask.'

'Okay.' There's plenty more I could say, and question, particularly her use of the pronoun 'we', *and* her rather loose job description, but I bite my tongue.

Suddenly the spring is back in Chloe's step, her eyes eager and wide as she spoons a thick layer of nutty spread over an equally thick slice of bread then hacks it in half with the knife. 'What's the most important thing in the world, to you? Apart from this amazing sandwich.'

I ponder this for a moment. 'Family, I guess, and friends of course.'

'Love,' she says, blood-red jam now dripping from the wagging blade. 'We're nothing without love.'

'You're screwed then, aren't you?' says a voice from behind. 'Nobody likes you.'

'Kiss my ass, bitch!' Chloe doesn't look up from her sandwich making duties.

A figure slopes past me, face buried deep within a pulled-up hoodie. A hand reaches for the sandwich.

'No!' Chloe smacks the back of the hand with the flat edge of the knife. 'That's for me and Lyra. Make your own.'

She turns to me and rolls her eyes. 'Just ignore him, he's an idiot.'

Without turning to me he extends a hand. 'Jackson,' he mumbles dutifully.

'Hi, I'm Lyra.'

'I guessed.' He wanders to the fridge, takes out a carton of orange juice, and gulps it straight from the carton.

'You hungover again?' asks Chloe, now clearly goading him. 'Where *were* you last night, Jackson? And what exactly was it you were doing?'

Jackson glares at her, an unspoken argument flashing between them.

'Well, it's nice to meet you,' I offer in an attempt to douse the tension.

Jackson looks in my direction for the first time, though his face remains impassive. He's handsome in a classic way; clean-shaven, strong jaw, thick, dark hair and unnaturally bright green eyes. 'Welcome to the shit show,' he says, which gives me an eerie sense of déjà vu.

'Happy to be here,' I say jokily.

'That won't last long, believe me,' he replies. 'You want my advice? Run for your fucking life.'

'What was all that about?' I ask when Jackson is out of earshot.

'Nothing, he's just a jerk,' says Chloe, now performing chest compressions on my sandwich. 'I did warn you about him.' She surveys the finished article. 'I might have cut the bread a bit thick. Told you we should have asked Marie.' Despite her jokey manner, there's a slight tremor in her voice.

'It'll be grand.'

Chloe dumps the sandwich in my hand.

'Jesus. It looks like a Scooby snack,' I joke, wondering how the hell to get my teeth around it.

'A what?'

'Scooby snack.' I ball my hands into fists. 'Lemme at 'em! Lemme at 'em!'

'Huh?'

'The dog? Shaggy?'

Chloe shakes her head.

'Doesn't matter.'

'You're kind of weird,' she says with a frown.

'You only just realising?' I bite into the brick, but the mishmash of peanut butter and jam turns my stomach. It's either that, or the sinking feeling that the Warrens aren't going to be the all-singing, all-dancing American family I'd hoped for. Though why would they be? Clearly something was badly wrong for Dee to take her own life. I swallow a mouthful of chewed-up mush and pray it stays down.

'You don't like it, do you?' Chloe dumps her uneaten sandwich onto the chopping board. 'I'm useless, aren't I? I wanted everything to be just perfect.' She suddenly bursts into tears.

'Hey, don't cry?' I awkwardly put an arm around her shoulder. 'I do like the sambo, honestly.'

Chloe looks at me, confused, then buries her face into my chest. 'I don't even know what you're saying Lyra, you make no sense.'

'Sambo. Sandwich.' I throw in some shushing noises, but the sobbing only intensifies as does her embrace around my neck. 'Look, please don't cry. It'll be alright.'

'It's not that, it's him, Jackson the asshole, I hate him.'

'He did seem a bit of an ass,' I try. 'In Ireland, we'd say he was an *eejit*.'

Chloe laughs through her tears. 'Eejit, I like it.' Pulling away, she takes a deep breath and wipes her eyes. 'He's an eejit alright.'

I gently stroke back the damp strands of golden hair stuck to her flushed cheeks and to my surprise feel an almost motherly tenderness. What is it about this girl that breaks down my barriers?

'Sorry for crying.' She sniffs, rubs her swollen eyes and forces a smile. 'I bet I look a mess.'

'Least you're not wearing eye makeup like me. If I cried, I'd look like Ghostface.'

'Who?'

'You know, the Scream thing?'

'Oh, the painting. Munch?'

'Sure.' I don't admit I was referring to the 1996 slasher film. Jesus, this kid doesn't half show me up.

'When was the last time *you* cried, Lyra?'

The question catches me off guard. 'Oh, I dunno, a while back.'

'When your boyfriend left you?'

'Erm, no, I don't think so.' I avert my eyes, panic now creeping up into my throat.

'When then?' she persists.

My head starts to spin as Chloe runs through a half-dozen occasions that must have made me cry; 9/11, banging my funny bone, stumping my toe, when Harry married Meghan, the ending of that 'super-emosh' film, *The Fault in Our Stars*.

'Honestly, I don't remember.' My fingers begin to tingle.

'Surely when your mom died?'

I feel like the airs been sucked from my lungs.

'Lyra? You alright?'

I'm saved from answering by the slam of the front door followed by the jangling of keys.

Chloe's eyes instantly brighten. 'Bill!' She claps her hands like a hyperactive child. 'He came home early. Come on.' She grabs my hand and pulls me to the hallway. 'You're gonna love him.'

Chapter Ten
Bill

Bill hears Chloe's chatter from the kitchen. There's only one voice, but from the rambling, he knows she's trying to impress, and that only means one thing – her guest is here.

He checks himself in the wall mirror, inspecting every minute detail of a face he knows has grown old and weary over the last three years despite the expensive eye creams, moustache dye and dentistry. Chloe's babble draws closer, and he quickly practices a smile. It'll have to do.

'Bill!' squeals Chloe from the living room doorway. 'Lyra's here!' She leaps down the hallway steps and wraps herself around his waist. Bill looks up to see a punk with bright orange hair, torn jeans and a tattoo – make that tattoos. She's the exact opposite of what he expected an author to look like.

He tries to resurrect the smile but it's gone. 'Bill Warren,' he says with an outstretched hand.

The punk clomps down the steps in army boots and shakes his hand.

'Lyra. Nice to put a face to the voice.'

She looks anxious. Like she feels out of place. Which obviously she is. *Why would anyone choose to dress down like that?*

'Amazing place you have here, Bill,' she says, then frowns. 'You don't mind me calling you that, do you? I don't know how it works over here. Mister Warren? Is that better? Jeez, I'm shit at this... sorry. Didn't mean to swear.'

'Don't be silly, Lyra,' interrupts Chloe. 'Of course you call him Bill.'

'It's fine,' confirms Bill. He untangles himself from Chloe and smooths down his shirt.

'I've been showing her round. *And* I made her something to eat,' says Chloe, beaming at Bill like she wants a pat on the head.

The punk speaks again. 'It's incredible! Bit different to my gaff back home. My whole house could fit in just your kitchen.'

Bill isn't sure what reaction she expects so just nods.

'Bet your house is full of interesting stuff though, yeah?' jabbers Chloe. 'Books you've written, poetry, photos, old letters...'

'Clutter, you mean?' The punk laughs. 'Yeah, you're right there. How do you keep this place so neat?' she asks Bill. 'With two kids and everything.' She gestures towards Chloe. 'Must have them well trained, eh?' She winks at Bill.

He flinches. The punk just winked at him!

'Oh no, wait, you've got Marie, right? Memory of a sieve, me.' The punk puts two fingers to her head likes she's shooting herself. Bill wonders if she's finished talking yet.

God, it's going to be a long two months, he thinks.

'I'll show you the guesthouse... where you'll be staying,' he says, trying to instil some usefulness into the conversation. 'After you.' He holds the door open and gestures for the punk to pass. Chloe immediately springs to her side and links arms but Bill places a firm hand on Chloe's shoulder, giving it a gentle squeeze. 'Go and ask Marie to bring some fresh towels for our guest while I show her around.'

'Oh, okay,' she says, disappointed.

'Sweet Jesus!' exclaims the punk as they cross the lawn at the side of the house. 'You have a pool!'

Clearly Chloe hasn't given Lyra specific details of Dee's death, thinks Bill. He sincerely hopes it remains that way. 'Chloe and Jackson are keen swimmers,' says Bill. 'Do you swim?'

'I know how to... if that's what you mean. Can't say I'm very good at it, mind. Schoolmates used to say I swim like an epileptic rhino,' she laughs.

'Maybe Chloe can give you some lessons,' says Bill, refusing to acknowledge the humour.

'That'd be cool.' The punk points at the house beyond the pool. 'Who lives there?'

'Nobody. That's the guesthouse.'

She stops walking, her eyes on Bill's, trying to work out if he's serious. 'You're having me on, right?'

Her disbelief brings a smile of satisfaction to Bill's face. 'I haven't been inside for a few months, so I've no idea what state it'll be in, but I asked Marie to freshen it up.'

'So nobody uses it now?' asks the punk, still flabbergasted.

Bill shakes his head.

'You're seriously telling me I've got all that to myself?'

'Dee had her library in there, and occasionally Jackson has friends staying over but he won't while you're here.'

'And Chloe? Did she have friends over?'

'Hmm. Let's just say Chloe is a little short on friends.' Bill pulls the door open for her and steps aside.

'Wow,' she says, looking inside. 'That's me moved in for good then.' The punk laughs.

Bill doesn't.

'Is this Dee?' She lifts a framed photo from the mahogany desk.

'Yes, on our wedding day.'

'I didn't see any photos of Dee in the main house,' she says.

Bill lets out a sigh. 'No, Chloe still gets upset if she sees pictures of her mom, so I moved them all in here. She knows where they are when she's ready to look at them.' He doesn't say that he'd rather not discuss the mental wellbeing of his step-daughter with someone he's known for barely twenty minutes.

'She's taken it really badly, hasn't she? I imagine it's not easy for you either.'

'I'll leave you to unpack,' he says, ignoring the question. 'Anything you need...' He turns to leave, then turns back. 'I need you to do me a favour.'

'Sure,' she says, replacing the photo on the piano.

'Dee's passing... it's still very... raw, especially to Chloe. She's an intelligent girl but she sees her mom's passing as a rejection of her. It's difficult for her to grasp depression and the like. So please don't bring the subject up with her... I need her to focus on the future, not dwell on the past.'

'Erm... sure. Though sometimes it's good to talk...'

'Not about this,' he snaps, then immediately tries to lessen the tension with a half-smile. 'Dinner is at eight.'

'To be honest, if you don't mind, I'm just going to sort a few things out and hit the sack. All that travelling... you know?'

'Of course, I completely understand. Would you like me to get Marie to bring you a light supper to eat here?'

'No, really, I'm good,' says the punk. 'It's just my bed I need right now.'

'Well, sleep well, and we'll see you tomorrow at some point.'

Leaving the punk to unpack, Bill heads back to the main house and crosses paths with Marie along the poolside. 'Just dinner for three, tonight Marie. Our guest is tired.'

'Oh, okay. Shall I take these in?' she asks, holding a neatly folded pile of towels.

'Yes, she's still unpacking at the moment.'

'I'll give her a hand then,' says Marie. 'She's lovely, isn't she? Lyra I mean. A breath of fresh air.'

'She seems... okay.'

'If anyone can get through to Chloe, I think she can.'

Bill notices Marie's raised eyebrow and takes it as a warning shot.

Chapter Eleven

Lyra

Well, that was awkward! Clearly, Bill hadn't Googled me before my arrival nor is he blessed with Marie's - what did she refer to it as – 'gift from God'. I'd have been more offended if the disapproval had come from a man who *didn't* sport a porn star moustache and cat-eye contacts.

Heaving my suitcase onto the King-size bed, I pull out a pair of Harry Potter pyjamas. Bold lettering on the nightshirt reads *Don't let the muggles get you down*. Kind of apt I'd say. Sod Bill Warren, and Jackson too, the judgemental eejits. Despite my inner-pep-talk, I can't shake the feeling that I'm out of place here. For sure, the location is stunning, a haven in which to write, and Chloe is super sweet, but the Warren's are clearly a family on the verge of collapse. How can I help Chloe through her grief if I'm banned from mentioning her mother?

With a head full of thoughts, I shamefully shove my discoloured underwear to the very back of a dainty brass-handled chest of drawers. The last thing I want is the state of my smalls lowering the tone amidst such sophistication.

On top of the chest of drawers lies a diamond-encrusted, framed photograph of Dee and Bill. The two are cuddled together on the bow of a motor yacht, their faces flushed with sunshine and possibly champagne which they're clinking together in crystal flutes. They look sickeningly in love, gazing at one another with the kind of passion I've only read about in Jane Austen novels. I pick up the frame and trace a finger over Dee's toothy smile. *'Lunar tides have left it dull, once a gleaming sight. Now battered, misused, and null, lost in the ocean's might,'* I whisper, my heart aching for this beautiful, broken stranger. 'What did you mean by that, Dee?'

A tap on the door makes me jump. 'Only me, *Bonita*. Mind if I come in?'

Quickly I place the photo down and make a strange throaty noise which roughly translates to 'yes.'

'You okay? You look like you've seen a ghost.' Marie stands in the doorway, the lower half of her face hidden behind a pile of pristine white towels.

'No, no, I was just...' I'm stuck between the drawers and bed, in no man's land. 'Just unpacking.' If awkward has a voice, I'm personifying it.

'I'll just put these in the ensuite if that's okay with you?' says Marie, crossing the room.

'No, please, I can do it.' I gesture for the towels, but Marie is having none of it.

'You should have let me unpack for you,' she chastises. 'I'm *your* housekeeper as well you know.'

The idea of ordering Marie around doesn't bode well with me and I tell her so.

'Come on, scootch up,' she orders, the towels now dispensed in the bathroom. I move halfway up the bed, but she chooses to sit shoulder-to-shoulder with me. 'I'm guessing this is a much different world to what you're used to, right?' she says, giving my thigh a reassuring squeeze.

I laugh. 'You could say that. Fish out of water springs to mind.'

'Well, just remember *I* only work here,' she says, tapping her finger on her blouse for emphasis. 'I'm not one of *them*.'

'Bill didn't like me,' I admit, surprised to hear the disappointment in my voice. A few minutes ago, I'd have sworn blind I didn't care what Bill Warren thought of me but obviously I do. The realisation is hard to swallow.

'He's just a bit... old fashioned, shall we say,' says Marie, and not unkindly. 'You know he tried to make me wear a uniform when I first took this job.' She chuckles. 'I humoured him at first, asked him to show me what he had in mind.'

'And?'

Marie makes a face. 'Hideous. Think Alice in *The Brady Bunch* and you wouldn't be far off.'

I don't recall ever watching the show, least of all what the housekeeper wore.

'All I'm saying, Lyra, is that whatever Bill's opinion of you, it's not important,' she continues. 'He's always going to be rich, but he's not always going to be right.' She offers a conspiring wink.

'He asked me not to talk to Chloe about her mother,' I say, feeling the need to offload.

Marie stiffens. 'I know,' is all she says after a pause.

I shoot her a look, but I can see she's uncomfortable, so I don't push the issue. I assume she's going to get up and leave, or change the subject, but neither happens. We sit in silence for a moment, but I can sense she wants to talk. 'You know you can trust me, right? I can keep a secret.'

Marie glances at me, as though weighing up if I'm sincere. 'As I said earlier,' she says cautiously, her voice dropping to a whisper. 'There's more to Dee's passing. I feel it.'

I think of the bottle still swathed in bubble wrap in my case and realise neither Bill nor Chloe have asked to see it yet. Surely that's odd? I know if it was a message from my mammy, it would be the first thing I'd want to read. 'How did Dee... you know?'

Marie visibly shudders. 'Knotted her ankles together with one of Bill's ties and threw herself into the swimming pool. Post-mortem found that she was high on drugs and drink, God bless her soul.'

'That's awful so it is... but you think there's more to it?' I press after some time has passed.

'I don't know. But I'll tell you this,' says Marie. She glances at the open bedroom door before turning her attention back to me. 'You mustn't say anything, to anybody, ok?'

I nod.

'I've only been with the Warren's since Dee's passing. There was another housekeeper before me, Gloria.'

'Oh.' This comes as a surprise. Marie seems to know the Warrens very well. 'So, you didn't know Dee?'

'I did yes,' she says, now gazing far off into the distance. 'The last housekeeper, Gloria, well she was a friend of mine, so she suggested to Dee that I cover her vacations or if her child was sick, which he frequently was. Gloria adored Dee and I soon realised why. I promise you, she was such a beautiful person.' She looks up at the ceiling fan and crosses herself. 'The strange part is this. When Dee took her own life, Gloria disappeared too.'

I weigh up what Marie is saying. 'Maybe she quit?'

Marie shakes her head. 'That's Bill's story but I don't buy it. I knew Gloria well. No way would she have given up the job here. Everybody knows the Warrens pay the best money. Most housekeepers on the Vineyard would sell their souls for this position.' She sighs heavily. 'She was a single mother with a, shall we say, special child. He lived with his grandmother while Gloria was a live-in here.'

'So, what then? You believe Bill sacked her?'

Marie shrugs. 'He says she couldn't handle the grief when Dee died, but I can't imagine she'd have been so devastated she'd leave. She was sad no doubt, but she'd been with Bill and Jackson long before Dee and Chloe arrived. And was she really devastated enough to leave her family without an income?' Marie throws me a look that says *not in a million years*. 'I tried to track her down just after Bill offered me a full-time position but seems she's vanished off the face of the earth. The grandmother still lives in Edgartown as far as I know but she no longer has the child.'

'Would it be an idea to visit the grandmother and just ask her where Gloria is?' I suggest. 'If it's bothering you so much?'

Marie considers this. 'I've thought about it. I know the address. But I'd be worried about Bill finding out and I need this job. The good Lord never saw fit to bless me with a husband or children, but I do have elderly parents to take care of and this position pays better than anything else around.' She rubs her eyes and I notice for the first time how exhausted she looks. 'Besides, Chloe needs me, I need to stay here for her, and Jackson too, bless his heart.' She crosses herself once again. 'He's a troubled soul that boy.'

'How so?'

'His mother walked out on him when he was a baby. I think he blames himself.'

I remember Chloe saying as much. 'How could any mother do that to their child?'

'Beats me,' says Marie quietly. 'He's tried endlessly to find her over the years but it's as though she's vanished off the face of the earth, too.'

'My mammy died,' I admit. 'When I was eleven. So, looks like all three of us have something in common.'

Before I know it, Marie has me wrapped in her arms. '*Mi Bonita*. I'm so sorry for your loss.' She kisses the top of my head.

For once I don't feel the need to pull away. 'It's okay, it was a long time ago.'

'Well, I promise you, she's not suffering anymore.'

My stomach clenches. I don't talk about *how* mammy died to anyone. 'How did you know she was suffering?'

Pulling back, Marie places both hands on my cheeks and smiles knowingly. 'Remember, I know things. She's at peace now.'

I swallow hard.

Marie's lips turn upwards but her eyes betray them. 'Right, I best get on, dinner to cook,' she announces. 'If you need me, don't hesitate to call.' She gestures to the phone beside the bed. 'Just press 1, that's my direct number; snacks, drinks, laundry, whatever. The fridge is full and I'll be coming in every day to tidy the place... but anything else, just call.'

'Okay,' I say, knowing full well I won't. 'Oh, and one more thing.'

'Anything, *Mi bonita*?'

'Do you know the date Dee died? I know Chloe said it was around six-months ago, but I just wondered.'

Marie nods. 'It was January 7th. Her and Bill's third wedding anniversary. Makes it even more heart breaking if that's at all possible.'

I feel a creeping unease at this latest revelation. Dee wrote the note on January 1st. Just six days earlier. Now I'm more convinced than ever that the poem was in fact a suicide note.

'Anyway, I have errands,' says Marie, signalling an end to the conversation. 'Remember to pick up that phone if you need me.'

With Marie gone, I wander through to Dee's library, remembering the trove of first editions I'd spotted on the way in. I need a distraction from the dark images now plaguing my mind. Poor Dee. How helpless must she have felt to kill herself in such a brutal way. My mind soon turns to mammy and within seconds, I'm trembling all over.

I sit down at a huge mahogany desk positioned by the window. A seasick feeling has come over me and I know that if I don't find a way to calm down, I'll suffer a panic attack.

Opening the desk's top drawer, I sift through an array of pens and highlighters and pull out a single page print out detailing houses and apartments for rent in New Bedford. Two properties have been highlighted - a run-of-the-mill two-bedroomed flat and a slightly grander two-bedroomed house with a garden. *Strange.* Neither property seems like something the Warrens would be interested in renting. And why would they? Bill could buy both houses with his loose change. It's only as my eyes rest on the *Move in* date that a thought pops into my head. Both properties were available from January this year. A line from Dee's poem turns my stomach: *Dreaming of breaking free, a star, from depths where currents twine.*

What if the poem wasn't a suicide note after all. What if Dee was planning to leave Bill? And if so, why would she then kill herself? It doesn't add up.

Stop with the Nancy Drew act, I think. It's real life, Lyra, not *Nancy's Mysterious Letter.*

I put the paper back exactly where I found it and open the second drawer. A stack of photos have been bundled together with an elastic band. The top one is of Chloe and Jackson, taken two or three years ago if I were to hazard a guess. Chloe is beaming at the camera, a ridiculously large fish dangling from a hook in her outstretched hand. Jackson has his arm slung around her shoulder and is pulling a shocked face, presumably mimicking the startled fish. They look happy, like typical siblings sharing a great adventure. When did it all go so horribly wrong for them? It was clear from their exchange in the kitchen that they don't like each other, and that's putting it mildly.

I take out the bundle and flick through them. There's half a dozen scenic ones, beaches and sunsets mostly, then a few more of the family. I feel a range of emotions as I scan through each one; mostly sadness that Dee is no longer here, that her life was cruelly cut short. She appears so vivacious, or at least she does in the earlier photos. In the most recent ones, where Chloe looks much like she does today, Dee has become a different person; her facial features buried under rolls of fat. She must have gained four stone, at least. Perhaps the most shocking of all is the flat look of hopelessness in her eyes. I run my thumb gently over her forced smile. 'What happened?' I whisper. 'Why did you feel you had to die?'

The final photo sends a jolt down my spine. I look again, more closely. It's a wedding photograph of a much younger Bill, his hair dark brown as opposed to the boot polish black of today. The moustache is absent and he's gazing at a bride dressed in white. I can see by her lean figure and the olive skin of her arms that it isn't Dee, therefore it must be Bill's first wife, Jackson's mum. My eyes fixate on her face, or rather the lack of it.

Somebody has scratched at it until it's been obliterated.

Chapter Twelve

Chloe

Hearing footsteps outside her bedroom, Chloe quickly replaces the floorboard and grabs a book from the shelf.

'Only me.' Bill stands in the doorway. He runs his eyes up and down her, finally settling on the book she's holding. '*The Perks of Being a Wallflower*,' he says. He saunters in and sits on the edge of her bed. 'Haven't you read that one already?'

Chloe thinks quickly, her heart hammering as she notices the partially raised floorboard. *Please don't let him see.* 'Yeah, I like it. I get Charlie, he's like me... a wallflower, I mean,' she clarifies, not wanting to anger her stepfather.

Bill nods. 'Better than being like Sam or Patrick, I suppose.' He strokes Chloe's bare knee. 'Patrick's a faggot and she's a whore.'

Chloe nods.

'So, our guest won't be joining us for dinner. Jetlag,' says Bill by way of explanation. 'So don't you be going over there disturbing her.'

'But...' Chloe's heart sinks. 'I only saw her for a few minutes.'

'And you'll see her again tomorrow,' he says, his tone implying there's no room for negotiation. 'And Lovebug...' he adds, now standing. 'Remember what we spoke about. Lyra wouldn't understand the complexities of love and the things we do for it,' he says kindly.

Chloe mimics zipping her lips. 'I promise.'

Chapter Thirteen
Lyra

I wake suddenly, heart pounding. In the silence I lie still, the nightmare seeping away like sand in an hourglass: If my conscious mind is the upper chamber and my subconscious the lower, then sleep is the hand that flips the device, and dreams are the filter between the two.

The night mammy died comes as snippets of memory; a teddy bear dangling by my side, my feet as cold as ice pops. *'Mammy, wake up, please.'* I think I spoke this out loud, but I can't be sure.

I sit upright against the headboard and refocus my mind on the present. Moonlight glowing through the partially opened window sketches the room in shades of charcoal. When I was younger, the darkness offered up beasts and ghouls to my overactive imagination but these days I enjoy it, the night like a blanket cocooning me from the stresses of the day.

I climb out of bed and pad across the deep pile rug to the window. Framed between two tall oaks, the water's edge gently rises and falls on the sandy beach like the breathing of a sleeping giant. A million nightlights glimmer in the onyx above, each distant and belonging, their significance sealed in time. Alone in this quiet, colossal beach house, three thousand miles from familiarity, I feel I'm the only living thing in the world awake. And then I see I'm not.

The sound of raised voices draws my attention to the main house. Two figures stand close together on the porch, silhouetted in the dazzle of a floodlight above an open garage door. I shield my eyes to see. They're both male, so I assume it's Bill and Jackson, though I could be mistaken.

The taller of the men is speaking loud enough for me to hear his voice but not what he's saying. I tease open the window a fraction more.

'I never should have agreed to it.'

This comes from the taller male, whose voice I recognise as belonging to Bill.

I strain to hear the other man's reply as he's speaking too quietly. The word 'cops' breaks through, as does 'Chloe.'

'Just get rid of her, Jackson! However you need to.'

Christ! There was no mistaking that. Who the bejesus is Bill talking about? Me? Who else could he have meant? I try to convince myself that I've heard it wrong, or at the very least I don't know the context of the conversation. Though neither reassurance stops me from fretting that I'm somehow in danger.

Chapter Fourteen
Lyra

'Wow!' Chloe stands in the porch, gawping at me.

'Is something up?' I blink sleep from my eyes and wonder what time it is. Over her shoulder, a mist blankets the ocean, the air still and silent save for the stereo bickering of birds deep in the oak and cedar trees. Unlike me, she's already dressed, her hair neatly braided into twin plaits.

'Your face, Lyra!'

'What? What's wrong with it?' I instinctively touch my cheeks.

'You've no makeup on! Weird. You don't look like you.'

Jeez, Is that all? From her horrified expression I thought I'd broken out in hives or something. I laugh. 'Sorry, should've warned you I look ghoulish in the morning.'

'You look ghoulish all day,' she says, deadpan. 'But it's better. You're prettier without, more like a lady.'

I refrain from rolling my eyes, knowing that line is straight out of Bill's mouth. The thought of Bill makes my stomach churn. Why does he want Jackson to get rid of me? It crosses my mind to just up and leave; I could make an excuse about needing to return home, but where would I go? Tom's now back in the house, no doubt with his floozy, and I carved out this time to find somewhere to live, not to mention write another book.

'What's your natural hair colour?' Asks Chloe, breaking my thoughts. She brushes past me and heads for the kitchen.

By the time I catch up with her she's busy emptying out the contents of the fruit bowl onto the countertop.

'It was blonde.'

'Cute. Like mine then. Do you paint your eyebrows on too? There are so many different shapes aren't there?' She continues while skinning a banana. 'When did you start with all the goth makeup? Do you want a smoothie by the way?'

I stifle a yawn. 'Way too many questions for this time of the morning, Chlo. And no, not for me thanks.' Still bleary-eyed, I rummage in the cupboards in search of caffeine, but a packet of organic roasting beans confirms my suspicions. 'No instant?'

'Instant?'

'You know, coffee granules? In a jar?'

Chloe frowns

'Doesn't matter. And I was around fourteen,' I add. 'When I started to identify with the Emo crowd.'

Chloe throws the banana and a handful of strawberries into the blender and wipes her hands on her denim shorts. 'Why them? Aren't they like depressed and have no friends?'

'Exactly why I relate to them,' I say, jokingly. 'No, it was the music at first. It really hit home, after mammy, you know...'

'Died?'

I force a smile. 'Yes, died. Actually, when mammy was alive I was more of a hippy like her. Flowers in my hair, all that jazz. She always encouraged me to not conform.'

Chloe looks up, her brow furrowed. 'But really she was influencing you to conform to her ideals, as a non-conformist.'

'No. Well...' I shrug, red faced. 'Like I say, this is all a bit much pre-caffeine.' I turn my back and examine the space-age expresso machine from all angles. 'How does this work?'

'Beats me. 'Hey, I've an idea!' Chloe's voice elevates to a squeal. 'Dye your hair blonde, like mine. I'll lend you some clothes and we can go shopping today. I can tell people you're my older sister! I've always wanted an older sister. How awesome would that be?'

I feign a laugh while tugging at a tiny, pull-out drawer on the coffee machine.

'So will you?'

'Will I what?'

'Your hair! Shall we go to the salon today? Get rid of that weird orange.'

'Err, no thanks, I like it like this. Besides...'

The fruit blender screams in protest as Chloe slams her hand on the button.

Feck. I've offended her. 'I've upset you, haven't I? About the hair thing.' I say, as the cacophony stops. 'I don't want to sound ungrateful, but I like my hair this colour.'

A sneer twitches at the corner of Chloe's mouth but she's quick to suppress it. 'You just do you, hun.' She turns her back on me and pours two tall glasses of creamy-pink froth.

'I said I didn't want one.'

'Well, you're not getting that espresso maker to work anytime soon, are you? Anyway, I want you to have breakfast with me. I've made Marie do an extra special one for you.'

Half an hour later, and looking very 'unladylike,' I make my way to the main house for breakfast. The door has been left ajar so, after a courtesy knock, I follow the aroma of hot coffee and salty bacon to the kitchen.

'Wow! Now *that* is a slap-up breakfast.' The table is swamped with an array of morning goodies; cream cheese and smoked salmon bagels, crispy bacon, a huge stack of pancakes laced with maple syrup, cereals, jams, croissants, decanters of juice and, *thank you Mother Mary*, a steaming pot of coffee.

Bill's beady eyes appear over the top of a broadsheet. He's seated with Jackson to his right and Chloe to his left. The image reminds me of Da Vinci's *Last Supper* - if Jesus had access to Botox and Cheerios, that is.

'Slap-up?' Bill speaks as though he has something unpleasant in his mouth. 'Sounds like something quite violent.'

Chloe gestures for me to sit at the chair opposite.

'Sorry. I meant the breakfast. It looks lush.'

'Lush?'

'Lush, you know? Grand?'

When Bill remains clueless, I feel my cheeks burn. Jackson glances up at me, shakes his head and smiles. His eyes are swollen from sleep, or more likely the lack of it.

'Nice. It looks nice... and huge.' I laugh to cover my embarrassment. 'Sure, you guys don't know half of what I'm saying do you?'

'I'd say that's a fair analysis,' states Bill, though he does pour me coffee so I decide he's not a total eejit.

'Is Marie joining us?' I ask, feeling somewhat vulnerable without her calming presence.

Bill gawps at me as though I've just suggested I take a crap in his fruit salad.

'Marie's our housekeeper,' states Chloe matter-of-factly. 'She doesn't eat with us.'

'Right.' I gnaw on a slab of cinnamon toast, but it sticks to the roof of my mouth.

'Did you sleep well, Lyra?' asks Bill, who on closer inspection looks pretty knackered too; dark bags hang under his eyes and his skin has a sallow hue to it.

'Not so great. I was up and down to be truthful. Jetlag messing with me probably.' I throw a glance over at Jackson and then to Bill to see if they react, but neither flinch. 'So, Chloe says you work for your daddy, I mean father, Jackson?' Trying to make small talk is not one of my best skills admittedly, but I'm keen to find out more about him. Aside from what went on last night, there's a certain mystery behind those bright-green eyes and elusive manner.

He throws a quick glance at Chloe, a forkful of pancake suspended between table and mouth. 'That's right.' His voice is gruff, as though laced with sandpaper.

'When he bothers to show up,' adds Bill, his mouth tightening into a frown.

'Me and Lyra are hitting the stores,' interrupts Chloe excitedly. 'Clothes shopping.'

'Lyra and I,' corrects Bill. 'Perhaps you can both choose something suitable for the function next week.'

'Ooh, a party. Am I invited?' I ask. Parties aren't really my thing, but nothing that a few glasses of wine can't make bearable.

'It's a black-tie evening, for a foundation I run,' says Bill.

'Oh.' I hope that didn't sound as disappointed as I feel.

'There'll be some very influential and important people here in our home, so it goes without saying that I expect you all to present yourself accordingly.' I swear he runs his eyes the length of me. 'Take Lyra to Stina's, Chloe. Use the card, no limit.'

Chloe's eyes light up. 'You hear that, Lyra? No limit!'

'Tomorrow we'll all go to the Aquinnah cliffs,' he continues, addressing us all as though it's a board meeting. 'It was one of Dee's favourite places, and I thought it would be a fitting location to read her letter together.'

My chest tightens at the mention of the poem. How will the Warren's react to it? Will they see something between the lines that I'm missing?

On my way to the guesthouse, I bump into Marie.

'How was breakfast, *mi bonita*?' She cups my face in her hands and kisses my cheek.

'Beautiful. Incredible in fact. I really hope Chloe didn't demand you did all that for me.'

Marie chuckles. 'She so wants to please you.'

'I'm being taken shopping today,' I say, making a face. 'I get the impression I'm meant to buy something ladylike for the charity thing next week.'

Marie raises an eyebrow. 'Filthy rich folk dressed in diamonds outdoing each other on who can be the most charitable. I've been given the day off, thank the Lord.'

'Yeah? I'd have thought Bill would want you on hand?'

She shakes her head. 'He brings a team of professionals when he hosts.' She emphasises the word *professional* with air quotes. 'Plus,' she leans in close, 'I don't think he wants me getting too close to the socialites. Some know too much about Bill Warren, and not all of it is charitable.' She leaves the statement hanging. 'It's my day off tomorrow,' she adds when I don't fill the silence. 'I'm going to visit Gloria's mother, see if I can track Gloria down and find out exactly why she left so suddenly.'

'Good for you,' I say, putting my hand on her shoulder. In that moment I feel more of a bond with Marie than with my hosts, which feels wrong and ungrateful somehow. After all, it's the Warrens who have given me a place to stay, paid for my flight and are now going to buy me clothes. But it's only Marie who I feel I can talk openly with right now. 'They've asked to see the letter that was in the bottle,' I blurt out. 'Only, there's an issue.'

Marie tilts her head to the side.

'You got a moment?' I gesture over to the guest house. 'I think you ought to read it.'

Chapter Fifteen
Lyra

I SIT IN SILENCE AS MARIE READS THE POEM, WATCHING her eyes for signs of surprise. When she's finished, she places it on her lap and smiles.

'Well?' I ask.

Marie shrugs. 'Not what I expected. To be honest, I don't really understand it.'

You and me both, I think. I'm sure Chloe will be able to shed some light on it, but at what cost to her mental health? 'I could be wrong, but...' I hesitate.

'Go on,' says Marie.

I wonder if I should offer up my suicide note theory, but after finding the property print outs in Dee's desk I'm angling more towards Dee wanting to leave Bill. 'It reads to me like she was planning to leave Bill. Here, this line.' I run my finger over the words as I read aloud. '*Dreaming of breaking free, a star, from depths where currents twine.* I think Dee was using the bottle as a metaphor for herself.'

'I'm sorry Lyra, I'm not so sure I understand,' says Marie.

'She wasn't really talking about the bottle but herself. Here, look at this line. *Lunar tides have left it dull, once a gleaming sight, now battered, misused, and null, crushed in the ocean's might.*'

When Marie continues to look at me with a bemused expression on her face, I explain further. 'Dee wasn't really talking about the bottle here. Or at least it was a double meaning, a metaphor… basically she was talking about herself,' I clarify. 'She's saying that she was once beautiful, but after being battered and abused she feels…crushed…or depressed. I think the Ocean's might is referring to Bill's temper…or his power…though of course the Ocean's might could signify depression and breaking free a star possibly signifies dying.'

Marie blows out a long breath. 'Perhaps she should have just said what she meant.'

Despite the situation, I laugh. Though of course that's the beauty of poetry, it can be interpreted in many different ways. 'I found a printout in the desk drawer,' I say, feeling compelled to reveal everything to Marie now I've begun. 'Somebody, likely Dee, had been looking at properties in New Bedford. Two had been highlighted, two bedrooms only.'

'That could be anything,' says Marie. 'Bill's a property developer.'

'Perhaps. But these two had a move-in date of January. Honestly, Marie. I think Dee was planning to leave Bill and the poem was perhaps a legacy of what she was planning to do because she knew how dangerous it was going to be. Seems coincidental that she ends up dead just seven days later don't you think?'

A frown creases Marie's forehead. 'What are you suggesting? That she didn't kill herself?'

I raise an eyebrow. 'You said yourself something was off.'

'I just meant with Gloria leaving so suddenly. Like she might have known more about why Dee died by suicide. You're insinuating she was…killed.' Marie's voice has dropped to a whisper. 'That's quite a leap. And anyway, she left a suicide note.'

'There was a note?' This is news to me. It also fully disproves my theory about the poem being the suicide note. 'What did it say?'

Marie shakes her head. 'I never saw it. I just know there was one.'

'And are we sure Dee wrote it? Was the handwriting the same?'

Jeez, Lyra. What are *you insinuating here?*

'Like I say, I didn't see.'

I wander over to the window and look out to where Bill is sunning himself on the porch. 'She was miserable with him that's for sure. I also found some photos in the drawer. The contrast in her appearance from her wedding day to just before she died is shocking.'

'They always seemed happily married to me,' says Marie. 'Though I didn't see them so much.'

'But Gloria did.' I turn back to face Marie. 'You need to track her down. We need to ask her some questions. And we ought to try and get our hands on the suicide note. At the very least we should check that the handwriting matches up to this letter.' I can barely believe what I'm insinuating and I wonder if I'm letting my imagination run away with me. Though surely the line- *gather each fragment, one by one, and hear its tale forlorn,* is a plea to look beneath the surface.

'I think we're creating something out of nothing,' says Marie, as though reading my mind. 'It could be dangerous, meddling like this. Why risk it? You didn't even know Dee.'

'I just feel something doesn't add up,' I say, knowing I'm only telling a half-truth as to why this matters so much to me. 'I don't believe she was anywhere near giving up.'

'And it's nothing to do with your own mother's suicide?'

My mouth drops open. 'How did you...'

'I know things remember.' Marie taps the side of her head. 'Your mother took her own life, didn't she? Something you still refuse to accept.'

'I really don't want to talk about it.' The words stick in my throat. The truth is I don't believe mammy would have intentionally left me. Besides, the cause of her death was a heroin overdose and mammy wasn't a user. I think it was a murder made to look like suicide but nobody has ever looked beneath the surface. I can't fail Dee in the same way mammy was failed. 'But no,' I say to Marie a little too forcefully. 'Needing to understand the truth about Dee's death isn't about mammy. Things just don't add up. Not just this poem but the print outs and the way Bill is adamant I can't speak to Chloe.'

'Okay,' says Marie, now giving my knee a gentle squeeze. 'Let's not get ahead of ourselves. I'll track down Gloria and we'll find out why she left.'

Chapter Sixteen

Lyra

I glare at the keyboard in disgust. An array of jumbled words stares back. I still have no idea what I'm going to write about, let alone how I'll top the success of *Mother*.

'Fuck you, all of you,' I say out loud and close the laptop lid. I'm talking to hardware, always a sign I need a break from writing.

Outside, the weather is as indecisive as me. Slow-moving clouds devour any remaining patches of blue one-by-one, leaving the sky completely overcast and sullen. I look around, wondering where to go and settle on exploring the grounds some more. Maybe there'll be some secret garden behind a hidden door, something that might breathe life into my current desert of creativity before I go shopping with Chloe this afternoon.

I step from the open lawn into the dense cluster of trees at the bottom of the garden and a sound of fluttering immediately catches my attention. I follow my ears to the source.

'Jesus, you made me jump,' says Jackson. He's stood inside a black, roofed cage the size of a large garden shed. It stands in the shade of a circle of tall oaks. Jackson has his arm outstretched as a rainbow of green, blue and yellow birds fly from one side of the cage to the other. One lands on his hand, snatches a seed and retreats to one of half a dozen perches hanging from the roof.

'Wanna come in?' Jackson points to the door with his eyes.

I can't say I've ever been a lover of birds. Pigeons freak me out, even more so the seagulls that swoop and scream over Gratton Beach. But I know that stepping out of my comfort zone is exactly what I need to kickstart my writing right now.

'I didn't know you were into birds?' I say, gently closing the wire meshed door behind me.

'Not mine, dad's,' he replies in a hushed tone.

I immediately duck as a colourful commotion breaks out over my head, the birds panicking at the presence of a stranger. I let out a small scream.

'Sssh, you're scaring them,' he says calmly.

'I'm scaring *them*?' I shelter behind Jackson's back.

He pulls more seeds from his pocket and peels back the fingers of my clenched hand. 'Here, show them you've got food.' He holds my wrist as I extend my arm as far from my face as I can. Straight away a tiny ball of moss green and royal blue lands on my palm. I whimper as it cocks its head then pecks at my skin.

Jackson laughs. 'He knows you're one of his own. That's a European finch.'

Stupid though it sounds, I feel strangely fortified by the fact that the bird is from my part of the world. Jackson puts another seed on my hand. This time a larger bird flies down, its face bright red and its breast neatly sectioned with mauve and yellow. 'Wow, that's beautiful,' I say.

'He sure is.' Jackson flashes a smile at me. I feel my cheeks flush. 'Gouldian finch,' he continues. 'Dad's favourite.'

The bird twitches its tiny head from Jackson to me, then back again, all the time chirping incessantly in tiny peeps.

'Never stops talking, that one,' says Jackson.

'Reminds me of your sister,' I say with a smile.

Jackson laughs. 'They've got a lot in common... always seeking attention, cute one minute, aggressive the next, and yes... never shuts up.' The bird eventually flies off, still chattering, and we both stand for a while, watching. 'Stepsister by the way,' says Jackson, breaking the silence. He throws me a look which says, thank God.

'You two have a strange relationship.'

'Me and Chlo? Yeah, we have our ups and downs. We used to get on better, when Dee first married dad, but she changed.'

'How do you mean?'

'I dunno, I guess she was all sweet and innocent at first, a normal kid I suppose, but then she kind of switched, went quieter, more withdrawn. Started with her weird shit.'

'Weird shit? Like what?'

Jackson bites his lip, as though realising he's said too much. 'Just went strange, it doesn't matter.'

More multi-hued birds break from the flock to take food from Jackson's hand. He names each type as they land, showing off his avian knowledge; 'Zebra. Star finch. Masked.'

'Dee, do you know why she was depressed?' I ask.

Jackson screws his face up. 'No idea. Why do you ask?'

'I just wondered if something had triggered it. Or someone,' I add, attempting to sound indifferent but failing abysmally.

Jackson's expression is unreadable as he processes what I've just said. 'She married a multi-millionaire,' he quips. 'Went from a two-bed apartment to a mansion with a private beach. That woman was given the world. Nobody triggered it.'

'Sorry, I wasn't suggesting...'

'Good. It wouldn't be wise to.' He looks me hard in the face.

'I'm sorry, I didn't mean to pry...anyway, I'll catch you later.' I try to leave but Jackson makes no attempt to step out of the doorway. Something strange is going on here. An unspoken argument. 'Thanks for showing me the birds.'

Jackson offers a courteous nod before moving out of my path.

I hurry out of the aviary, wondering what the hell has just happened.

Chapter Seventeen
Lyra

Considering it was supposed to be Chloe taking *me* to buy a dress, she seems to have won by about 15-2 when it comes to shopping bags. A pair of heels and a fancy frock for me, a whole new wardrobe replacement for Chlo. Still, it was fun, and we got to hang out together away from the house.

'Do you like oysters?' she asks, somewhat randomly as we stroll arm-in-arm down Main Street.

'I'm from Galway. I was weaned on shellfish,' I say, smiling.

'Let's eat here. We can get an ice cream across the road after.'

Chloe stops and stands in the doorway of a cosy looking restaurant. 'You'll have to get the door.' She holds up her multitude of shopping bags apologetically.

An oversized American flag and paintings of boats hang from the redbrick walls in the dark, industrial-like interior. Three men stand behind a bar that extends the full length of the building. All wear identical ZZ-Top beards, black t-shirts and flirty smiles as their eyes follow our entrance. A lone diner makes no effort to contain his staring too.

Chloe flings her bags under a wooden table and shouts over for two coke floats. 'That okay with you?'

I nod and sit beside her. A vodka and orange would have been better, but I'm just glad to take the weight off my feet; this girl shops like she talks – incessantly.

Chloe insists she orders for us both, and within moments paper placemats are slid onto our table along with Chloe's murky drink of choice.

The other diner still hasn't taken his gaze off me, and nervously I start fidgeting with the placemat, folding one corner to another, then ironing down the crease.

Chloe laughs; 'What you making?'

'I don't know yet. It's origami. My mammy taught me. Helps calm me down.'

Chloe watches for a while, slurping on her drink through a straw. 'I can't wait to go to the cliffs tomorrow, to see mom's letter.'

I look up. 'Really?'

'Of course,' says Chloe matter-of-factly. Perhaps seeing my confusion she adds, 'At first I didn't know if I wanted to read what she had to say. I was angry at her for a long time. But now you're here, I'm happy. I think mom sent you to me, so now I forgive her.'

My throat tightens. 'I can understand why you'd be angry. But Chloe.' I force myself to look at her in the eye despite my cheeks burning. 'You need to prepare yourself.'

'How so?'

'Your mom, she wrote a poem. And it's a little... well, it'll be interesting to hear what you make of it,' I say, suddenly tongue-tied.

'Cool. Mom loved poetry. We had our own little poetry club, just me and her.' Chloe slurps again.

'I imagine you miss her a lot.'

'Yeah, it's kinda weird her not being around,' she says through a sigh. 'Though she was hard to live with by the end.'

'In what way?'

'Just down all the time. Nothing seemed to make her happy.'

Still keeping my eyes on the paper-folding, I decide to casually sneak in a direct question. 'So, how did she seem to you the day she... you know?'

Chloe looks at me for a moment, eyes wide, lips pursed around the straw. 'The day she killed herself?

'Yeah. If that's not too personal a question.'

I catch a flash of something in her eyes. 'She was sad, as always. Bill bought her a beautiful necklace for their anniversary, a solid crystal heart. But I caught her crying in the bedroom just after. She yanked it off and the chain snapped.' Chloe shakes her head. 'I don't know why she would do that. It was a such a neat gift. I have it now,' she says, fishing it out of her collar.

She isn't wrong. The pendant looks heavy enough to sink the Titanic. 'Did you ask her why she'd yanked it off?'

'No. She told Bill it just snapped, that it must have been faulty. He didn't believe her either though because I heard them arguing about it later that night.'

'What was being said?' I wonder if I'm asking too many questions, but Chloe doesn't seem in the least bit fazed.

'He was calling her ungrateful. She was slurring something about wanting to feel her own heart, not a dead-weight around her neck. She was oiled,' she adds, rolling her eyes. 'She didn't make much sense a lot of the time.'

'How did she die?' I know this already of course, but I want to see if Chloe will offer any further details.

'She drowned... in the pool,' she adds in a quiet voice.

I do a fair job of acting shocked. 'But how do you know it wasn't an accident? Especially if she was hammered.'

Chloe relays everything Marie has already told me, though claims to not know what Dee used to bind her ankles. 'I didn't see her. It was Bill who discovered her and called the cops.'

'And did she leave any note? A suicide note?' I add when Chloe frowns.

'Oh... yeah. It was all a bit bizarre though. Some half-baked poem.' Chloe swallows. 'She sure liked writing poems. Bill has it somewhere. I only read it the once. Just a lot of self-pity and nowhere near her best work.' Her eyes suddenly light up as the waiter approaches. 'Ooh, oysters. They're here. I wonder if we'll get a pearl. Do you know how you can tell if they've got pearls in even before you open them?'

And before I can press her any further, she's off on some old wives' tale about shell markings and a hundred other incredible facts about oysters, and then the moment has passed, for now at least.

Chapter Eighteen
Lyra

Our leisurely stroll along the Aquinnah Cliffs is a far cry from the mad dash of yesterday's shopping trip. Chloe and I walk side-by-side through yellow-flowered gorse and heather high above the white sands of Moshup Beach.

'Isn't it so awesome?' Chloe links my arm tighter, so much so that we're in danger of tripping each other up and falling arse-over-tit down the cliff. 'You can see, like, forever. Don't you find that so liberating, Lyra, like there are endless possibilities?'

'It's true, and that's why I couldn't live anywhere but by the sea. Anything else just seems so claustrophobic. What do you reckon, Jackson?'

'Huh?' Jackson looks up from his phone. He's beside us physically, but a thousand miles away in his head.

'The view. Does it make you feel free?'

Jackson glances out towards the hazy outline of what Chloe told me are the Alexander Islands and the Rhode Island shoreline beyond. 'Not really,' he mumbles. 'Makes me wonder why I can't get a phone signal here.' He holds his phone at arm's length and turns in a circle. I'm all for mobile technology and the like, but jeez, in such a stunning place it seems sacrilege to not appreciate these views. He's probably seen it all a hundred times before, mind.

Bill stands at the cliff edge ahead of us, watching the Atlantic rollers cascade onto sand and rocks a hundred feet below.

'Did you know that the red streaks come from the blood of whales?' Chloe bends down and runs her fingers over the terra-cotta clay. 'Moshup the giant dragged them from the beach and ate them.' She peers up at me and grins. 'Or so legend has it.'

'They were formed by glaciers millions of years ago,' adds Bill, squinting in the bright sunshine. 'They erode pretty badly though so don't go too close.' This he directs at Jackson who seems to have found his signal and is angrily stabbing out a message from the very edge of the clifftop. Jackson throws Bill a tight smile but doesn't move any further back. It occurs to me that I've been with the Warrens for three days now and I still know virtually nothing about Jackson. And the slashed photograph of his mother in Bill's desk drawer is still very much a mystery – who would do such a thing?

Chloe stands and dusts off her bare knees. 'Yeah, move back Jax. Wouldn't want any accidents, would we Bill?'

A flicker of emotion crosses Bill's face. Anger? Fear? I look from him to Chloe and then to Jackson.

'We'll head to the lighthouse and then eat at the inn. I've booked a table,' states Bill, his lips now bone white. 'Move away from the edge Jackson, I won't tell you again.'

We continue the trail in fraught silence. Despite Bill's warning, Jackson is still ambling dangerously close to the precipice. From my vantage point he looks as though he's one step away from falling to his death. He looks agitated, repeatedly stuffing his hands in and out of his jean's pocket and throwing nervous glances over at Bill.

'What are you thinking about Lyra?' Chloe slides her arm back through mine and leans her head on my shoulder.

That I don't trust your stepfather and brother. 'Nothing much, and you?'

'About Mom. We loved walking this trail when we first moved to Chappy.'

'Where did you live before? I don't think you've ever said.'

A wistful smile kisses Chloe's lips. 'New Bedford. Mom grew up there.'

My stomach lurches. So Dee *was* looking to move back home. It makes perfect sense that she'd return to somewhere familiar. 'Do you think your mum missed living there?' I ask, my voice catching.

Chloe peers up at me, a flash of memory reflecting in her eyes 'Yeah, she loved it. We both did. It's the setting for Moby Dick you know.'

'Sounds incredible.'

Chloe's shoulders sag. 'We were pretty poor though. My biological father walked out on me when I was a baby so Mom was working two jobs to pay the bills. I was on my own a lot.'

'I know that feeling.' A heaviness bears down on me as I remember the endless lonely nights of my childhood, my only company a bunch of fictional characters in the dusty hardback books that mammy once read aloud to me.

'How did your mammy and Bill meet?' I ask, sensing that Chloe is eager to talk. Bill's warning to not discuss Dee with Chloe is still at the forefront of my mind but I've decided that he has no right deciding how she should handle her grief.

'A charity event. Mom was waitressing there.'

'Love at first sight?'

She shakes her head. 'Hardly. She was a bit of a hippy, like your mom I guess.'

'Yeah?' I remember the photos in Bill's desk drawer of Dee, presumably not long after they'd met. She was dressed in long-flowing dresses and beaded necklaces. 'Did she change a lot when she married Bill then?' I know I'm prying but Dee's poem is playing heavy on my mind, especially as I know the purpose of this trip is to read the damn thing.

'What do you mean, did she change a lot?' asks Chloe.

I word my answer carefully. 'I meant, did Bill disapprove of how she dressed? Did she change because of him?'

'Bill saved us,' snaps Chloe. 'We were nothing without him, a pair of down and outs.'

'Do you really believe that?' My tone is harsher than intended but I'm beginning to get sick of Bill Warren's bigotry. It's obvious that such a derogatory term has jumped right out of his mouth and into Chloe's.

'Bill's an amazing man,' states Chloe defensively. 'He only wants me to be the best version of myself.'

'I'm not saying he doesn't.' I root around for the right words, aware that with Dee dead and no blood family to speak of Chloe will be reluctant to say anything negative against her stepfather. 'All I'm saying is that you can be who you want to be, not what Bill or anybody else expects you to be.'

'Like you, you mean?' I hear the sarcasm in her voice.

'Well not an emo... unless you want to be of course.' I smile in an attempt to lift the mood.

Chloe stares straight ahead, her eyes fixed on the lighthouse up ahead. 'But Mom never should have married Bill.'

My ears prick up at this. 'Why do you say that?' I grab hold of her hand and feel the tension in her wrist and fingers. 'It's okay. You can trust me.'

'Because they were bad together.' Chloe's voice has dropped to a whisper. 'She wasn't happy with Bill. She hated this life and wanted out of it.'

I don't know if Chloe is confirming her mother wanted to leave Bill or if 'wanted out of it,' is reference to the suicide.

I know the question needs to be asked. 'Chloe, are you certain your mother took her own life?'

Chloe looks taken aback. 'Of course she did! Why would you even ask that?'

'I ...don't know.' I suddenly want the ground to swallow me up. 'Ignore me.'

'I will!' Her voice is suddenly razor sharp. 'Seriously Lyra, stop looking for drama where there is none. If you want the truth, I hate mom for what she did. There, I said it! She was nothing but a selfish bitch!'

Chloe storms off in front, leaving me trailing behind. We don't speak again until we reach the lighthouse where we dutifully listen to Bill as he drones on about its history; the year it was built, it's subsequent rebuild, how the earliest lighthouse keeper was the first white male to reside on The Vineyard, etc. etc. He pats the exterior red and white stones of the lighthouse like he's greeting a college buddy. It's very clear to me that Bill suffers from sophomania, believing himself to be more intelligent and knowledgeable than everybody else.

'Don't show even the slightest interest or he'll never shut up,' breathes Jackson in my ear. His face remains enticingly close to mine.

I suppress a smirk, relieved that yesterday's 'misunderstanding' seems to have been forgotten. 'Take it you weren't jumping for joy at coming here today?'

Jackson makes a face. 'I could think of a hundred better ways to spend my Sundays.'

'Like?'

'You like live music?'

'Course. Well, if it's decent.'

'There's a new rock band playing tonight at The Loft. You're welcome to tag along if you like?'

'Erm, sure.' I'm taken aback by this sudden show of friendship.

'Keep it between us two, though. Meet me round the back of the garage at eleven.' Jackson's bright green eyes glisten with mischief. 'We don't want hangers-on, do we?' He gestures to Chloe who's nestled into Bill's chest, his arm draped around her.

'So Lovebug, it seems the time has come to read your mother's words, don't you think?'

Feck! Despite knowing that the moment was coming, I'm terrified to show them the poem. Each line stabs at my heart; *Harken to the bottle's plea. Take it gently, don't delay. Set its spirit free.*

I wonder if I ought to hold off showing them. At least until Marie has spoken to Gloria.

'This lighthouse was your mom's favourite spot you know,' I hear Bill saying to Chloe. 'It was here that I first told her I loved her.'

Chloe abruptly pulls away. 'Can we have the note now Lyra?'

I hesitate. 'Erm, sure.' I make a show of rooting around in my rucksack. *Just give them the note, Lyra, this isn't your decision to make.* My fingers curl around the bottle. 'I...erm...'

'You haven't forgotten it have you?' asks Jackson, laughing awkwardly when I don't reply. 'Say you haven't?'

'Erm.' I look up at the three of them, each displaying a unique expression.

'Lyra?' Chloe's lip begins to tremble. 'Where's the note?'

'Lyra?' Bill's eyes blaze fury.

The remnants of its glassy shell,
Hold truths of the deep.

There's more to Dee's death, I know it. I failed Mammy, I won't make the same mistake with Dee.

'I'm sorry.' The lie on my tongue burns like hell. 'I left it in Ireland.'

I don't know what reaction I was expecting, but Chloe threatening to jump from the cliff, isn't it.

Chapter Nineteen
Marie

Marie raps on the flaking, pale-blue door frame then smooths out the creases in her floral dress. First impressions are vital. Her mother drilled that into her from the first day at Sunday school.

After a few seconds the door opens as far as the safety chain allows.

'Who is it?' says a face peering through the gap.

'Darlene? It's Marie. I'm a friend of Gloria's.'

'She's not here.'

'I know.'

'How do you know my name? What do you want?'

'I want to talk to you, *mi amor*.'

'What about?'

'About Gloria... and the Warrens.'

'Are you the police? The papers?' Darlene's voice elevates with each question.

'No, I'm a friend,' says Marie, keeping her tone purposely light. 'We worked together, me and your daughter. I work for the Warrens now.' Marie waits while the old woman processes this information. 'I've brought you some fresh donuts from Back Doors,' she adds, lifting the white box.

There's a rattle of chains from inside and suddenly the front door swings open. Darlene holds open the flimsy mosquito screen. 'You'd better come in then.'

Marie scans the interior, but the only light is from the flicker of a small television framing a game show host. As her eyes adjust to the dark, she sees that every surface holds the clutter of unwashed crockery, pages torn from newspapers, and framed baby photographs.

'Where shall I put these?' she asks, holding out the box of donuts.

'What are they?' asks Darlene, wiping her hands on a grubby plaid skirt.

'They're donuts.'

'I know, but what kind?'

'Oh. I'm not sure, my love, I just asked for an assortment.'

'Chocolate?'

'Yes, I'm sure there's a chocolate one in there.' Marie feels slightly awkward at the silence that follows. 'Shall I make us a nice cup of tea and we can have a look?'

Darlene nods.

'Where are your cups, honey?' says Marie through the open kitchen door. She clears enough space in the sink to fit the kettle under the tap.

'Shelf, next to the refrigerator.'

Marie chooses the two least-stained cups and drops a tea bag in each. 'It's a lovely house you have here,' she says, turning round. She notices the corners of Darlene's mouth lift slightly. 'Really… cosy,' Marie continues.

'It does right for me… and Miss Suzy.'

'Suzy? Who's that then?'

'Miss Suzy. My cat, of course.'

'Ah, of course.' Marie turns back to the sink and discreetly wipes a stain from a plate with the edge of her hand. She arranges the donuts on it and places it on a stack of trashy magazines by the side of Darlene's threadbare recliner. 'There, a chocolate one, especially for you.'

Darlene nibbles at the edge like she wants to make it last forever.

'May I?' Marie gestures at a hardback chair in the corner. 'I bet you miss Gloria living with you.'

Marie sips at the tea while she watches Darlene peck a neat circle around the chocolate frosting. 'Where's she living now? Is it far from here?'

'Can't tell you,' says Darlene without lifting her eyes from the donut.

A sickly knot lodges in Marie's throat. 'Why's that, my love?'

'Can't. Don't got to tell nobody.'

Marie nods, the gesture allowing her precious thinking time. She decides to change tact. 'Do you remember the day Dee Warren died; God rest her soul?'

'Uh-huh.' Darlene nods.

'What did Gloria say about it?' asks Marie. 'She must have been very upset.'

Darlene laps at the chocolate frosting like a cat. 'Was all shook up. Said she was never going back to that place.'

'Did she say what happened?' asks Marie, now barely able to keep her voice level.

'Said Miss Dee had died.'

'Are you enjoying that chocolate, sweetie?'

'Uh-huh.'

'Did she say how she died, Miss Dee, I mean?'

'Said she drowned. Did it to herself.'

'And did Gloria know why Dee might have taken her own life?'

'Said she had no idea why, but I knew she was lying. Her and Miss Dee were close. Miss Dee treated my Gloria good. Didn't look down on her like most.' Having stripped the donut of all chocolate, Darlene places it back on the plate and seems to ponder her next choice.

'Have that one.' Marie points at a vanilla-iced donut; 'They're lovely.'

Darlene picks it up and sniffs it.

'How could you tell she was holding something back, Darlene?'

'Just could. She jabbers in her sleep too. Always has. Kept saying *sorry Chloe, forgive me.*'

Sorry Chloe? Marie wonders what Gloria could possibly have been sorry for? What had she done to Chloe?

'And did you ask her what that meant?'

'Said she didn't know... said it was just a dream.'

'And then she moved out?'

'Only after he turned up. That Mister Warren.'

Marie feels her heart rate rocket. 'Bill?'

'No. The boy. Evil, just like his daddy.' Darlene looks away, lost in thought. 'My Gloria upped and left a day later with Bubba. Needed to move on, she told me. Broke my poor heart, it did.'

Marie places her hand on Darlene's. 'Aww, God bless you. That must have been so hard for you when she went to... where was it again?'

'Salem.' Darlene tests the new donut with the tip of her tongue.

'Darlene?' Marie cradles Darlene's hand with both of hers. She can sense she's close. It's now or never. 'You know I'm a very good friend of Gloria's, my love. I want to help her. You want me to do that, don't you, to help your daughter, and your Bubba?'

'Uh-huh.'

'You're a good mother, Darlene. Give me her address and I'll go and tell her how lucky she is to have a mom like you, such a beautiful person inside and out. I'll make sure she's alright.'

Darlene pauses mid-lick. She puts the donut on the arm of her chair, stands up, and pulls a slip of paper from a chest of drawers behind her. She hands it to Marie. 'Don't tell no-one else, specially that Bill Warren.'

'It's our secret, I promise.' Marie leans forward and kisses her on the cheek.

'And you shouldn't be working there no longer,' says Darlene.

Blood thunders in Marie's ears. 'Why?'

'Cos that poor woman was killed,' she says firmly. 'I might not have all me faculties, but you'd have to be a complete idiot to believe she threw herself into a swimming pool.'

Chapter Twenty
Lyra

'What in God's name are you doing?' Bill marches over to where Chloe is balanced on the lip of the cliff. 'Come away from there, now!'

'Fuck off!' Chloe's eyes burn with rage. 'Come any closer and I'll do it.'

Bill stops dead, his hands held out in front of him.

'We can get the note airmailed,' I add unhelpfully. 'It's not the end of the...'

'Be quiet!' Bill hisses at me, his eyes as hard as flint. 'You've done enough.'

'You forgot the note Lyra. It was all I had left of her.' Chloe's voice, so raw with pain, causes the truth to burn my mouth. Whatever my suspicions, I can't be responsible for her doing something stupid.

'Lovebug,' Bill's voice softens to little more than a whisper. 'We'll get your mom's note, I promise. Come away from the edge.'

'I miss her so much.' Chloe covers her face with shaking hands, her sobs seeping through splayed fingers. Her apparent love for Dee seems at odds with her earlier words, but I appreciate the poor girl will be feeling mixed emotions.

'Chloe, listen...about the note'

'She won't jump.' Jackson's words deflate the confession before it hits the air.

I turn to him, surprised when I see that he's cool as ice. He rolls his eyes at me. 'She's forever going off like this. Drama's her middle name.'

'She's just lost her mother,' I snap. 'Cut her some slack.'

Jackson scoffs. 'Whatever.'

'Chloe. I need to speak with you. I'm going to come to you okay.' Bill edges forward, his outstretched hand trembling. 'We can sort this. I promise.'

'She's dead because of me!'

A sickly knot presses against my throat. *What the hell is she saying?*

Jackson grips my upper arm. 'Come away. You don't need to be caught up in this.'

'In what?' I look him dead in the eye and see a flash of panic.

'Don't listen to what she says, she makes stuff up,' he garbles. 'Come on, best we wait over...'

'She didn't though, did she!' shrieks Chloe at Bill, causing both me and Jackson to spin around. *Shit,* what did I just miss? 'And now she's dead because...'

'Please Chloe, not here.' Bill looks over his shoulder at me and Jackson. 'Take Lyra back to the car,' he barks. 'Now!'

'No, she should know the truth.' Chloe looks over at me, her expression one of deep regret. 'Lyra, you need to know this. Mom didn't ...'

Bill lunges forward and grabs the collar of Chloe's sweater, yanking her back. They hit the ground. Chloe kicks out and screams obscenities as Bill restrains her.

Jackson runs over and drags Chloe off Bill, hissing something indecipherable into her ear.

Chloe breaks free. 'I'm tired of covering for you, too,' she shouts, her finger jabbing at Jackson's chest. 'And so was mom! You're disgusting!'

Chapter Twenty-One

Lyra

My eyes dart open. 'Shit!' Day has turned into night. I must have fallen asleep when I got back from the cliff outing, or should I say the cliff debacle! All I can remember is deciding to lie down for a few minutes to clear my mind from the day's craziness... and bingo! It's now... I look at the clock... ten fucking o'clock, five hours later. And I'm supposed to meet Jackson in an hour.

Despite the time, I dilly-dally in the shower, allowing the powerful jets to wake up my frazzled mind. I spend the minutes debating whether to meet Jackson tonight. On one hand, I'm too mentally drained for small-talk and ear-splitting rock music, but on the other, it might be my one time to grill Jackson about Dee's death. Chloe was desperate to admit something on the cliffs earlier, and I'm positive Jackson knows what it was.

Once out of the shower, I dry off, throw on my clothes, and adjust my face in exactly five minutes flat.

'Nice motor!' Unsurprisingly Jackson is a million miles away on his phone and I make him jump with the comment. He quickly turns over the screen then gives me a questioning smile. I'm not sure why. *Is he testing if I saw the message?*

'You onto your secret lover?' I ask with a straight face.

He pats the white leather passenger seat. 'Get in, we're late.'

'Late for what? It's a band. Are they waiting for us before they can start?'

Jackson smiles sarcastically. 'I've arranged to meet someone.'

I buckle up and we tear down the driveway in his black Mustang. I can't tell if he's trying to impress me with his driving, or if he's just angry I'm late.

Within minutes we're at the ferry quay. 'It's off the island, then?' I ask.

'The Loft? Yeah, of course. OB. Only nightlife on Chappy involves clam chowder and middle-aged cover bands... if you're lucky.'

I have no idea where or what OB is, but it all adds to the mystery. 'See, you *have* got a sense of humour behind that serious front,' I say.

He turns to me as we edge off the ferry and, at last, I get a genuine smile.

'You're popular,' I comment. Jackson, or maybe his car, is obviously well-known judging by the number of hands waved our way as we cruise through Edgartown before swerving off onto Beach Road. But, as is Jackson's way, he gives nothing away, only smiles knowingly.

The speedometer needle winds quickly clockwise as we speed along a sand-strewn road, the ocean glittering on either side. I put the window down and let my hand dance in the warm wind. It feels like I'm in a Hollywood road-trip movie, a far cry from driving in the rain along Galway High Street after last orders.

Usually, at this hour on a Sunday night I'd be feeding Tom from a polystyrene carton of chips and curry as he chuggs us home in fits and starts in his battered Ford Fiesta. Which reminds me, he was a shit driver, as well as a shit boyfriend His loss, I think, as I note Jackson's gleaming white shirt, expensive shoes, and tanned, manicured fingers clamped around the steering wheel of a Ford Mustang. A Mustang for feck's sake!

My mind flicks back to this morning at the cliffs. I turn to face Jackson. 'So, are you going to tell me what all that was about before?'

Jackson throws me a glance then turns back to the road. It's the first time I notice his profile; good bone structure and a chiselled jaw. He's not what you'd call model material, his nose is out of shape for a start, but he's a *dote*, as they say back home.

'Go on,' I urge.

He keeps his eyes fixed on the road: 'Ignore anything Chloe says. She's full of shit, loves a drama.'

'Behave,' I say, laughing in an attempt to keep things light. 'I'm not having that. She said I ought to know the truth.'

'Ask her then.'

'I did, when we got back. She said she didn't want to talk about it. I think she's pissed that I forgot the note. I don't blame her really, she'd...'

'Lyra,' interrupts Jackson, his hand now on my leg to quieten me. 'Chloe is a nasty piece of work. She likes to cause rifts, even in the family. It's just something she gets off on.' He turns to look at me. 'You *have* been warned.'

It's obvious he's not going to reveal anything about his stepsister. She's not straightforward, that's for sure. But I still don't accept it was something she said off the cuff, just for a reaction. I spend the rest of the drive looking out of the window and wondering if I'll ever unearth this family's secrets.

Chapter Twenty-Two
Lyra

At The Loft it's obvious I've judged the dress code badly wrong, again. While Jackson gets respectful nods from virtually everyone we pass as we walk in, I'm subjected to head-to-toe judgements that range from shock to outright disgust. It seems that a night of letting yourself go in this part of the world isn't the same as in Galway. For guys it means turning your shirt sleeves up and leaving your shirt unbuttoned at the collar. For girls it's about choosing your best pearls. For me it's about wearing whatever the fuck is comfortable - and grungy, so four-inch platforms, a tartan skirt and a ripped, black Slipknot tee-shirt is my fashion of choice. Obviously, it's not everybody else's.

There's only one other piercing on show apart from a range of conservative earrings, and that's in the nose of a pony-tailed barman trying to keep up with the demands of a three-deep throng eyeing up each other's designer labels at the bar. Naturally when feeling socially awkward, this is the place I immediately feel the need to gravitate towards.

'Shall I get us a drink,' I shout at Jackson above the music.

'Huh?' he shouts back. He looks over the top of my head, his attention elsewhere.

I stand on my tiptoes to reach his ear.

'I said... hello, I'm Lyra. Do you come here often?

He pulls away and looks at me, confused, the humour obviously passing over his head like the laser beams crisscrossing in flashes of red, purple and green.

I mime tipping a glass. The penny drops and he mouths the word *beer*. I weave my way through the throng of preppy party animals and wait my turn at the bar. The crowd emits a polite roar as the house lights dim and the band takes to the stage. Jackson is talking into the ear of a man dressed equally immaculately. With their perfect teeth, styled bed-head hair and expensive shirts, they look like celebrities. Having said that, everybody looks like a celebrity to me in here.

Jackson seems to be listening intently to what's being said, nodding and laughing sporadically. I wonder what they're talking about as I totter back with two beers, but the man sees me coming and disappears into the crowd before I get back.

'Who was that?' I ask nodding at the retreating figure.

The band burst into life, cutting short any chance of further questioning. As we watch them, the same man appears a few yards away and nods at Jackson to follow him. Jackson holds up five fingers to me and gestures for me to stay put before following the man deeper into the crowd.

Now, stood alone and exposed, more disparaging looks are thrown my way from clubbers making the journey from bar to band. Rather than stand here like the main exhibit in some kind of freak show, I decide to lose myself in the crowd nearer the stage. The band are surprisingly quite good, edgy without the pretension I'd expect from an act performing for this kind of crowd. Almost involuntarily, my body starts to move to the gut-punching drum rhythm and melodic, bass guitar melody. As the energy intensifies, I feel the urge to jump, to dance, to punch the air, to submit to this raw energy. It's the first time since arriving in America that I feel anything quite so primal and spontaneous. Until now, my experiences have all seemed so... manufactured and premeditated - fun-by-numbers, if you like.

The next song drives the energy up another notch, but before I let loose – and probably make an arse of myself – my eyes are drawn to two men to the side of the crowd. They stand in the shadows, out of the glare of the stage lights that twist and turn bouncing beams of colour against the vaulted ceiling and red brick walls. One of the men passes something to the other. That other man is Jackson.

Chapter Twenty-Three

Jackson

Jackson's ears are still ringing from Mad Circus as he trails Lyra out of the club. They were pretty diabolical in truth, too much ego and not enough talent.

'That was fun! Where next?' Lyra looks over her shoulder and flickers her eyelashes at him.

God damn it, that's all Jackson needs. No way was Lyra crushing on him part of the plan. All Jackson had wanted to do was get her on side. 'Home. It's late'

Lyra twists his wrist to check his watch. 'It's only 1.30. The night is young.'

'Some of us have work tomorrow.'

'Me too,' she says, slurring. 'I'm writing.'

'That's not working.'

She grabs his arm. 'Come on Jax. One more for the road, pleeeaase?' She turns down her mouth, trying to look cute.

Even though she's faking sadness, it shows Jackson a different side of her, a contrast to the tough bitch persona she's touting with her ripped clothes and piercings. He knows he could have said something before they left the house, asked her to change, but he kind of likes the fact she does her own thing, doesn't care what people think... or at least doesn't seem to care. He can only dream of that kind of freedom. For as long as he can remember he's always had to live up to other people's expectations, behaving how others want – a millionaire's heir, the perfect stepson, an upstanding member of the community, a representative of Bill's company. He knows how fast his dad would disown him if he knew what he really got up to. 'Come on, follow me,' he says with a resigned sigh.

Within half a block they're at the ferry docks, where they turn left. Jackson leads the way out over the water along the creaking, wooden Fishing Pier.

Lyra pauses. 'Don't you think you're taking me skinny-dipping, young man.'

He laughs to mask his unease. 'This is where I go... to think.'

'Oh, you think, do you,' she says, now barefoot and carrying her boots. 'You're full of surprises, master Warren.'

The night is silent save for the slosh of waves against the timber supports below as they sit dangling their legs over the side.

'So watcha thinking?' she asks, the two of them now gazing out to sea.

'Err... nothing really.'

'Come on.'

'Okay. I was thinking about mom. My mom, not Dee.' He cringes the moment the confession leaves his mouth. Still, if it bonds him and Lyra, then it's worth it.

'Ah, sorry. Chloe told me she left when you were wee.'

'Pardon?'

'Wee. Small.'

'Ahh, right.' Jackson likes the way Lyra talks, even if he doesn't understand what she's saying half of the time. She's quirky and a whole lot of awkward. If things were different, he'd probably try to get to know her on a more personal level.

'I don't know very much about mom. Her name is Whitney. She was twenty-one when she married dad and twenty-three when she had me. But that's it. I don't even know if she's still alive.'

Jackson can sense that Lyra wants to ask more so gives her the silence to do so.

'Have you never tried to track her down?'

'Yeah, a few times, a while back now though. I never got very far. Seems when she left she vanished into thin air.'

'And your dad can't help? Surely with his money and contacts he could track her down?'

'If he wanted to, maybe. He gets pissed if I so much as utter her name... I don't blame him...not really. What woman walks out on her husband and three-month-old baby?'

Deep down Jackson knows there'll be more to the story than a deadbeat mom. He witnessed how his father treated Dee when she was alive; it wasn't pretty. Although he doesn't blame Whitney for wanting a better life for herself, he only wishes she'd found the strength to take him with her.

'That's so shit. I'm sorry.' Lyra puts her head on Jackson's shoulder. He wonders if she senses him flinch. He can't let her get close, as much as he'd like that, it's too dangerous.

'Jackson?'

He doesn't like the way she says his name, a prequel to an awkward question. 'Yeah?'

'Who was that man you were with at The Loft?

'What man?' He turns away and coughs into his fist.

'When the band were on. I saw you with a man, at the side.'

'Just some guy I know.' The lie swells in the ensuing silence. 'Our dads are friends,' he adds, feeling compelled to give her a modicum of truth. 'But I don't know him that well.'

'You seemed to be doing some kind of business with him.'

As much as Jackson wants to be completely honest with Lyra, he knows there's no way she can find out about his 'extra-curriculars'.

He's relieved when she doesn't ask any more questions and

they resume their gazing out over the still waters of Oak Bluffs Bay. It's a comfortable silence, not awkward like Jackson usually finds it with most people. But as much as he likes Lyra, he knows that if she does find out who Brett really is, he'll have to find a way of silencing her. Just like he did with Dee.

Chapter Twenty-Four
Chloe

The night is the hardest time to be alive.

Chloe envies people who sleep well. Her mind is far too active for that. The dead of night is when her mind does its deepest thinking.

Tonight, she's considering whether to tell Lyra the thing she knows she mustn't. She pictures the moment her lips confess the truth and it both scares and excites her. She worries that Lyra would be angry with her for not speaking up sooner. What if she no longer wanted to be Chloe's friend? Lyra's the greatest friend Chloe has ever had, an expansion of herself and the true definition of a soulmate. If Chloe was ever going to tell anybody about what really happened the night her mom died, it would be Lyra.

But then...Chloe thinks about Bill, and her promise to him.

What's more important? Friendship or family?

She turns over to face the bedroom window. The starless sky is a visual silence, giving the question space to breathe. The stars, of course, are still there; light pollution has simply made them invisible to the naked eye. Chloe likes to think about her mother in such a way. Death has made Dee invisible, but that doesn't mean she isn't still there.

Car headlights announce Jackson's return. Chloe checks the time on her phone. 2.20am. Late for a Sunday. She wonders if he's been drink driving again and climbs out of bed to check. He's *so* irresponsible. Bill would kill him if only he knew.

Chloe presses her face against the window and watches as Jackson emerges from the garage. She loves to watch people when they don't know they're being watched; it's the only way to see them in their natural state.

Only Jackson isn't alone. The shock of who he's with causes Chloe to cry out.

She hurries back to bed and pulls the cover up over her head.

'Bitch,' she mutters, over and over. 'Backstabbing, Irish bitch!'

Chapter Twenty-Five
Lyra

'Good morning, *bonita*.' Marie wanders into the study carrying a basketful of cleaning products. 'All good with you on this beautiful morning?'

I quit circling the cursor over a blank Word document and swivel round to face her. 'The usual. Wondering how I ever managed to string two sentences together, let alone write a best-seller.' The aching in my skull, courtesy of last night's drinking, doesn't exactly help matters.

Today is my fourth day with the Warrens and I still haven't come up with even the seed of an idea, never mind a detailed story outline. My editor, Ian, sent me a shirty email this morning 'encouraging' me to send him sample chapters by the end of the week, just to see if I'm 'on the right track.' I'm not on any track. In fact, the track hasn't even been built.

'Come on Marie, give me a story idea, quick.'

'Hmm. How about a clairvoyant housekeeper who persuades spirits to dust and polish for her in return for communicating messages to their loved ones?'

I pretend to consider it. 'Good hook but where's the twist?'

Marie tickles me with a feather duster. 'The spirits were the ones making all the mess in the first place.'

I laugh. 'You're wasted in this job.'

'I know.' She takes out a clear spray bottle and douses the curtains in zesty lemon. 'Secret recipe,' she says, tapping the side of her nose. 'Half a cup of water, five drops of lemon oil, fresh lavender and a dash of vodka.'

'Not so secret if you tell everyone,' I tease.

'Talking of secrets...' Marie's voice drops to a whisper. 'I visited Darlene yesterday, Gloria's mother.'

'What did she say?'

'Bless her soul, she's in a bad way.' Marie crosses herself. 'I promise you, she has a beautiful heart, but I don't think she was at the front when the good Lord was handing out brains.'

'Did she give anything away about Gloria?'

'A little. Seems Gloria is in hiding, or at the least doesn't want to be tracked down. And get this.' Marie puts her mouth to my ear. 'Jackson visited her at home. The next day, she left. Gloria made Darlene promise to not tell anybody where she was living. She seemed very scared of Bill.'

I feel the blood drain from my face. 'None of this sounds good, does it?'

'This isn't your mess honey,' says Marie. 'Nobody would blame you if you decided to go back to Ireland.'

I shake my head. 'I'm going nowhere. If something untoward happened to Dee then I want to get to the bottom of it. I failed my own mammy. I'm not about to fail Chloe's.'

Marie stops spraying the curtains and crouches down beside me. She holds both of my hands in hers and squeezes tight. 'Why do you think you failed your mom?'

My eyes sting though I'm certain they'll be no tears. 'The Gar...the police,' I correct, 'they weren't interested in mammy. Just saw her as another deadbeat druggie. She did have her issues, but she never touched smack. I should have fought harder for her. Made them look into her death more closely.'

Marie's eyes search mine. 'You don't remember do you? Your mind has blocked the memory of the night she died.'

A hot flush of shame spreads through my body. 'I feel guilty. Like I could have done something, stopped somebody from doing something perhaps. But no, I can't remember.'

'She was mentally ill,' says Marie, now squeezing my hand. 'It was nobody's fault, least of all yours.'

'I wish I believed that.' My voice breaks but my tears stay jammed. 'What is your gut telling you about Dee?' I ask, keen to change the subject. 'You said you know things. So what do you know?'

Marie emits a sad little laugh. 'The problem is I never know the full story. Words, images, sometimes just emotions, they come to me as single jigsaw pieces but never enough to complete the puzzle. And not about everything,' she adds as an afterthought.

'Well just humour me. Do you honestly think she died by suicide?'

'I don't know,' admits Marie. She wanders over to the window and sighs. 'Darlene told me that Gloria was talking in her sleep the night Dee died. She was saying, *sorry Chloe*. What do you think she was sorry for?'

I join Marie at the window. I'm surprised when she rests her head on my shoulder. 'Did you get the address?'

'Yes.'

'Are we going to visit her?'

Marie nods. 'How about tomorrow? I'll phone in sick; you meet me down by the ferry port at eleven. Tell the Warren's you're spending a day sightseeing, by yourself.'

I can't imagine Chloe will take too kindly to that, but I agree, ignoring the part of my brain that's warning me not to get involved. 'I'll see you then.'

Marie quickly wipes a rag over the mahogany bookshelf then

packs away her cleaning things. 'Right, I'll leave you to it. If you do write about the psychic housekeeper, make me bright and beautiful.' She throws me a sassy smile.

'Oh, I forgot to tell you. Jackson took me to a club last night.'

Marie beams a smile. 'What, like a date? I promise you, he's a lovely boy, you'd make a handsome couple.'

I feel my cheeks blaze. 'God no! Nothing like that. We like the same music. I only mentioned it because of something I saw there.'

Marie frowns. 'Saw what?'

'Well, here's the thing.' I wonder if I'm adding fuel to an already raging inferno, but I trust Marie to keep it quiet. 'When we were at the club last night, Jackson disappeared. Then a while later I caught sight of him with a dodgy looking fella. I think he might have been drug dealing or something.'

Marie visibly gulps. 'No! Are you sure?'

I shake my head. 'No, I'm not. But on the cliffs yesterday Chloe blurted out that she was tired of covering for him and so was Dee. What if he's involved in something illegal?'

'Bill would go crazy. He'd see it as a smear on his own character. He's highly thought of in the community. No,' she shakes her head. 'Bill wouldn't like that one bit, he'd likely disown Jackson.'

I consider my next question carefully, not wanting to cause undue suspicion but knowing the possibility needs to be pondered. 'So, if Dee had found out that Jackson was drug dealing, do you think he'd have been worried?'

'Definitely,' says Marie. 'Jackson would have done anything to stop Dee telling his dad.'

Chapter Twenty-Six
Lyra

Before I know it, the sky is black and strewn with stars; a damning contrast to the clean-white page on my Mac. Another day of achieving very little, now over.

Calling it a night, I head over to the main house in time for dinner. Marie has promised an all-American banquet and having picked all day on crisps, or potato chips as Chloe insists I call them, I'm salivating at the thought. I still need to break the news to Chloe that I'm 'sightseeing' alone tomorrow; she'll not be happy but 'such is life', as mammy would say. Accompanying Marie to Gloria's house is important, not only to support Marie but, hopefully, to settle the sick feeling in my stomach that my hunch is right, that Dee Warren *was* murdered after attempting to leave Bill.

I spot Jackson heading into the aviary and go after him. Instead of surmising what he was up to at the club last night, I figure I'll just ask him straight out.

'Jax?'

He spins around, his eyes wide, as though caught with his trousers down.

'Shit, did I scare you?' I laugh, my eyes adjusting to the semi-darkness.

When he stays quiet, I think something must be wrong with him. 'Jax? You, okay?'

'Dad's birds.' It's only when he says this that I realise the aviary is silent. I edge closer to the cage and peer in.

'Jesus. Are they all…'

Jackson nods. 'Looks like they've been poisoned.' He opens the cage door and goes in, not indicating whether I should follow.

'God, this one's still alive.' He gently scoops up a trembling scrap of a thing and holds it out to me. My heart sinks as I realise it's the bluey-green European Finch. 'We need to call a vet.'

Jackson shakes his head. 'It's too late. Look, he's convulsing.'

Before I can say another word, Jackson has turned his back to me and I hear a tiny, sickening snap.

'You killed it?'

He nods mournfully. 'At least he's free now.' He crouches down and gently lays the bird back on the ground with the others. 'No living thing deserves to be caged.'

I have a sickening feeling that he isn't just referring to the birds.

Best I tell dad,' he says, sidestepping me. 'He's going to go mental.'

I trail Jackson back to the main house, unable to keep up with his stride. How the hell have a dozen exotic birds been poisoned? 'Jax, do you think somebody did this to them?'

He casts me a worrying glance over his shoulder. 'No idea. Maybe contamination in the water.'

'Ahh, *mi bonita*, I missed you today!' Marie wraps me in a hug the moment I enter the kitchen.

'Wow, now this is a feast!' The dining table is crammed with dishes of all colours and smells. A glass bowl overflows with salad leaves; a plump, freshly baked loaf sits on a wooden cutting board; steam rises from a casserole dish of gleaming, tomatoey meatballs; a pair of wooden spoons poke like TV aerials from a bowl of spaghetti that's surely enough to feed the five thousand; and all manner of sauces, dressings and dips colour any gaps in-between.

'I aim to please,' says Marie. 'How did the writing go today?'

'So, so.' I gesture over to Jackson who is whispering into Bill's ear. 'His birds are dead,' I mouth.

Marie's hand flies to her mouth '*Mi Madre*! How?'

The sound of a chair scraping across the floor, stops me from answering. I watch on as an ashen-faced Bill gestures for Jackson to follow him.

'What's up?' asks Chloe, glancing up from her book.

'Nothing for you to worry about, Lovebug,' says Bill, his voice unsteady. 'Your brother and I just need to go and deal with a little problem. Eat up,' he adds, gesturing to the banquet. 'Marie, set aside two plates please.'

'Will somebody tell me what's going on?' demands Chloe once Bill and Jackson are out of earshot.

'It's the birds,' says Marie softly. I watch as she goes over to Chloe and, bringing her hand to Chloe's face, gently runs a finger over her cheek. 'Seems they're all dead.'

Chloe erupts into an explosion of tears and flings herself into Marie's arms. 'Why does everything I love have to die?' she cries, her voice emanating from the depths of Marie's bosom. 'Everybody leaves me.'

I've never once heard Chloe mention her father's birds, so her reaction seems overegged, though it *is* typical Chloe. 'Hey, I'm so sorry,' I say, patting her shoulder. 'I can't imagine how...'

'Leave me alone Lyra!' Chloe pulls away from Marie and glares at me, her eyes as black as night. 'All you've done since you arrived is make things worse!'

Chapter Twenty-Seven
Lyra

'Chloe was *not* happy this morning when I said I was sightseeing alone,' I tell Marie as we approach a sign for Vineyard Haven. 'I didn't think she'd have been bothered after that carry-on last night. I've a good mind to just pack up and go home you know, though with Tom now in the house I've nowhere to go.'

'Is there no way forward for the pair of you?' Asks Marie, taking her eyes off the road.

'No chance. Did I not tell you I caught him screwing his secretary? In our bed!'

'*Mi Madre.* Men are useless,' says Marie. 'It's why I've never had one.' She throws me a sassy grin.

'I best get looking for a bedsit really. I can't imagine I'll be staying here the whole two months, not with Chloe hating on me.'

Marie squints at the Satnav on her phone, taking her eyes off the road once again. 'That's just Chloe's way. She'll have not meant anything by it, I promise you. Likely just emotional about the birds.'

'Do you think they were deliberately poisoned?'

Marie takes a sharp breath, cutting me off. 'The Warren's are a lot of things, Lyra, but they love animals.' She crosses herself, presumably on my behalf. 'Anyhow, Bill says they likely passed on some kind of disease to each other.'

'Well, I'm no vet but it seems weird that they all died at the exact same time. And Jackson did look shifty last night.'

'Jackson adored them!' interjects Marie. 'If I couldn't find him in the house, I promise you I'd find him in the aviary.'

I want to protest further but the Beetle suddenly judders to a stop. 'We're here,' she announces.

I glance down at the crumpled paper in her hand and then over at the numbered placard at the end of a drive that disappears into dense woodland. 'Yep. This is definitely the one. So, what do we do now then? Just go straight up and see if Gloria's in?'

Marie shrugs. 'Not much else for it.'

We traipse along the drive until we reach a clearing in the beech trees. Here, a dark wood cottage sits on a small, uncut lawn. As a home it's quite large and looks very cosy, like a giant treehouse, but its seclusion adds a sinister feel. It reminds me of the witch's house in the Hansel and Gretel story mammy used to read with me.

'I imagined a rundown shack, not this,' says Marie, hands pressed into her hips.

'I reckon I'd find my muse in a place like this. Wonder how much it costs to rent.'

'Much more than a housekeeper's wage that's for sure. So how in the Lord's name can Gloria afford it?'

We climb half a dozen wooden steps to the wraparound porch and stand at a half-open door.

'Leave me to do the talking, *bonita*,' whispers Marie. She taps on the wooden frame.

'Are we going to tell her about Dee's letter?'

Marie shakes her head. 'Let's see what she has to say first.'

Marie taps again. Within seconds a chubby boy of around six or seven bounds from the dark interior towards us.

'Who are ya? Cole like ice-cream. You got some?' He snatches the carrier bag out of Marie's hand and begins rifling through it. 'Cool! Twinkies.'

'Yes, my lovey,' says Marie, unflustered. 'They're for you. Is your momma at home?'

The boy doesn't appear to hear. He's too busy ripping the Twinkie wrapper with his teeth.

'Cole, who're you talking to, Bubba?' A middle-aged lady, who I assume to be Gloria, breaks mid-sentence. Her eyes dart between me and Marie.

'Hello Gloria.' Marie's voice is polite but authoritative. 'We need to talk to you.'

It seems an age before Gloria speaks, whether through shock or fear, I don't know. She's a tiny white woman, with paper-thin skin, protruding bones, and greying hair at the roots. I suspect an eating disorder of some kind, though the weight loss could be recent judging by the oversized sundress she's wearing. When Gloria finally finds her voice, I'm surprised at the anger that resides there.

'How d'you know where I live?'

'Your mother,' says Marie, holding her hand out when Gloria starts to protest. 'Don't go blaming her. She's worried for you. She misses you, darlin'.'

I watch the fury in Gloria's eyes shrink to sadness.

'What are you playing at girl?' continues Marie, friendlier now, but with a trace of disappointment. 'Why you left your mamma like that?'

'Cole, go to your room, Bubba,' says Gloria, her voice unsteady.

The boy leaves without protest, seemingly satisfied with his stash of goodies.

'You oughtn't have bought him all that junk,' states Gloria once he's out of earshot. 'He's too fat as it is. Wait there,' she adds, still standoffish. 'I don't want him hearing. We can talk on the porch.'

'So, what do you want?' she asks when the three of us are

seated around a rickety wooden table that overlooks the enchanted woodland. 'And who she?'

Marie smiles at me before answering. 'Lyra, from Ireland. She's a writer and she's staying with the Warrens for the summer.'

'A writer?' A flash of what I take to be disgust turns up Gloria's mouth. 'Like a reporter? I ain't being interviewed. Got nothing to say.' She folds her arms and turns away.

'That's not why I'm here,' I say, figuring that to gain Gloria's trust we're going to have to trade some sort of truth. 'I found a message in a bottle, on a beach in Ireland.' I pause. 'It was from Dee.'

Gloria doesn't outwardly react, but I notice the slight twitch of her nostrils. 'I came over to reunite the family with the bottle,' I finish, not wanting to show our hand completely.

'Such a shame what happened to poor Dee,' adds Marie. 'Must have been a heck of a shock for you, sugar.' I sense that Marie's choosing her words carefully to elicit a reaction.

Gloria hides her expression behind the rim of her teacup. 'Was.'

After a breath of silence, Marie places her drink down and leans forward. 'Gloria, we're friends, aren't we, me and you?'

Gloria blinks in quick succession. 'S'pose.'

'Lyra and I... we both feel there's more to you leaving your job so suddenly.'

'Ain't,' protests Gloria, far too quickly in my opinion. 'Just too upsetting is all.'

Marie nods and then takes her time to gaze at the bluebells and dandelions speckling the clearing. 'Beautiful place you have here. Real private.'

My gaze switches from Marie to Gloria, the tension now palpable. 'Bubba likes it,' says Gloria. 'Fresh start we needed.'

'Must have cost what, six-hundred thousand or so.'

'I got it rented. Got a good deal.'

'And are you working at the moment?' asks Marie.

Gloria visibly swallows. 'Here... there. Listen, what you want from me? I just want a quiet life, just me and Bubba.'

'The truth,' I state, more harshly than intended. Gloria backs away, her face full of fear.

'We want to know what really happened the night Dee Warren died,' says Marie softly. 'We believe you know more than you're letting on.'

Gloria starts to wring her hands. I'm even more certain now that she's hiding something.

'You gotta go now,' she mutters. 'Ain't good for my nerves. Cole, you know, he got problems.' She looks at me, almost pleading with me to cut her some slack. 'He not like other boys his age. Like my momma, he is. They both... special.'

Marie glances at me. *Go easy on her.*

'There's something else you should know.' I look at Marie for approval. She nods. 'The bottle that I found on the beach from Dee was written one week before her supposed suicide. It contained a poem. Here, see for yourself.'

I produce the poem from my jean's pocket and pass it to Gloria. Reluctantly she takes it and begins to read.

'All too confusing for me,' she says, handing it back. 'I never was the best at reading.'

'I think Dee knew her life was in danger,' I say, watching Gloria closely for any sign of guilt. '*Remnants of its glassy shell,*' I quote. 'And *set it's spirit free*. Seems to me that Dee knew that she'd be dead by the time the poem was found, or at least she feared she might be.'

Gloria's eyes swell with tears.

'Gloria, tell us, please,' urges Marie. 'Do you know something more?'

'Miss Dee, she was good to me,' says Gloria, at last. 'She didn't treat me like I was a nobody. She was kind, you know? But she was private, don't tell me much about her personal life ′n′ such.'

But living with the family, you'd have seen the goings on, right?' asks Marie.

'I saw enough.' The tremor in Gloria's voice is obvious.

'You say that like you saw things you wish you hadn't,' I say.

Gloria looks to Marie who nods her encouragement. 'You can trust us. Bill doesn't know we're here. Nobody does.'

'Okay...Mr. Warren... I guess he was... a little controlling of Miss Dee. But's that's all. I know nothing else.'

'Controlling how?' asks Marie, not missing a beat.

Gloria shrugs. 'Chose what she wore, what she ate, what friends she had. No different to most the men in those fancy houses, but I don't think Miss Dee could stand all that; she such a happy one when they first be married. And by the end... she nothing but a shadow.'

'No wonder she was ready to leave,' I fume. 'Misogynistic arsehole.'

'How do you know she was gonna leave?' asks Gloria, shocked. 'She told no-one that but me.'

So she *was* about to leave Bill.

'Why commit suicide if she was planning to leave him?' I say to Gloria. 'Surely you can see that's odd?'

Gloria tenses. 'I can't say no more. Said too much already.'

'Gloria, did you find something?' asks Marie, as though the thought has just come to her. 'Something bad?'

Gloria's eyes widen. 'Who you been talking to?'

Marie keeps her eyes firmly on Gloria but doesn't reply for the longest of time. 'We *are* going to the cops Gloria, with or without your help. We had our suspicions before, but you've just confirmed them. Now tell me what you found.'

Gloria chews on a barely visible thumbnail.

'Please,' I say, my voice catching in my throat. 'For Dee.'

I can't. Please don't bring in the cops,' she cries, grabbing hold of Marie's hand with both of hers. 'They go 'n' lock me up there ain't nobody gonna care for Bubba. Please Marie, just let me be.'

My whole body floods with fear. There's now no doubt whatsoever that there is more to Dee Warren's death.

'It's okay, *bonita*, no police.' Marie holds a now sobbing Gloria tightly to her chest. 'You just tell us what happened, it'll be alright.'

Gloria's sobs intensify, so much so that I can barely make out what she's saying but I think it's along the lines of Bubba needing her.

'And Chloe needed her mother, but she's dead,' says Marie, silent tears now streaming down her face.

How can everybody cry so bloody easily?

'Momma?'

The three of us glance back at the house to where Gloria's son is hopping from foot to foot, a puddle of pee at his feet.

'Bubba.' Gloria is on her feet and over by Cole's side in double quick speed. 'He always feels his momma's stress,' she shouts at us. 'Just leave us be!'

'Ok, we'll go now, honey,' says Marie, silencing me when I try to protest. 'You're right, Bubba needs you. Take my number though.' She takes a scrap of paper from her handbag and scribbles down her number. 'Put yours too,' she says, passing me the pen.

I jot down my number, unsure how I've become embroiled in a murder mystery in less than a week.

'I know you're afraid,' Marie is saying to Gloria, 'but Dee needs you. She needs you to speak up for her.'

'Find Chloe's diary,' says Gloria, now clutching hold of her son as if for the last time. 'I ain't saying no more than that. You'll find all you need in that diary!'

'What the actual feckety feck?' I strap myself into the Beetle's passenger seat. 'The poor woman's absolutely terrified!'

Marie puts the keys into the ignition but it's obvious she's in no fit state to drive. 'I didn't want to believe it. Poor Dee.'

'We need to go to the police. Tell them what we know.'

Marie shakes her head. 'We can't do that to Gloria. Bill will sweet talk the cops with that silver tongue of his and then she and Cole will pay the price.'

I blow out a frustrated breath. 'How did you know she'd found something?'

'It just came to me,' says Marie, accompanied by facial expression which says, don't ask how.

'The Lord sure moves in mysterious ways.' I playfully nudge Marie to lighten the mood. 'But you were right. There's a diary. Carry on with these insights and you might just make a believer out of me.'

'For we walk by faith, not by sight,' says Marie, raising her eyebrows at me.

'Perhaps so, but the cops are going to need a little more than faith if they're going to arrest Bill Warren. We have to find that diary.'

'And the suicide note,' adds Marie. 'If our suspicions are right and she didn't commit suicide, then the note is forged and won't match the handwriting of the poem. That, plus whatever is in Chloe's diary, should be enough for us to involve the police.'

Chapter Twenty-Eight
Lyra

'Hey, you're back. Wanna go for a walk?'

'Jesus wept, Chloe. You half scared me to death!'

'Thought you might want to hang out.'

'Oh, I can't,' I say, not having the mental vigour for her boundless energy. 'I've really got to crack on with this book. I've hardly written a word since I arrived.'

Chloe's face drops like a brick, from excitement to disappointment. 'You've already been sightseeing by yourself. *I* wanted to show you round.'

I can see she's genuinely hurt. 'It wasn't you. I just needed to clear my head, get some space... you know, for the book? It's a writer's thing. *You* know all about that, don't you?'

Chloe's mood lifts a little, obviously pleased at me considering her a fellow martyr of the literary arts. 'Sure, I know what you mean. Can I read what you've written so far?'

I instinctively cover the screen with my hands as she leans down to peer. Obviously, she *doesn't* know what it's like as an author. Letting someone read your work when it's only first draft feels like taking your clothes off in front of a complete stranger. Again, her face clouds over and I immediately feel a pang of guilt. I look at the half-filled page on my laptop, then back at her sad eyes, and sure enough, my trusty author procrastination kicks in. *Why waste a good opportunity to walk away from the thing that pains me?*

'I guess I could do with a break. Come on then.'

'Really?' chirps Chloe.

The changes in this kid's demeanour are like a light switch. She goes from one end of the scale to the other in a blink, rewarding those who turn on her brightness with a blinding ray of appreciation from those beautiful eyes and mouth. It's either just a natural trait, or she's one hell of a manipulator for a fifteen-year-old.

The beam stays on her face as we pace across the lawn and onto the sand. Suddenly, I feel her fingers intertwining in mine as she takes my hand. It feels... awkward, not least because it was only yesterday that she was accusing me of 'making everything worse.'

Chloe carries on talking as if it's the most natural thing in the world. I don't want her to feel rejected *again*, so I leave my hand there, but now all my focus is on my right arm. What's normally a subconscious movement, swinging my arms as I walk, now becomes a conscious effort because Chloe's swing is out of sync. *Do I let my arm hang loose to follow her movement? Do I take the lead? Jeez, why has walking become an ordeal?* I bend to pick up a stone and hurl it into the sea. Chloe doesn't seem to have noticed my deliberate escape as we continue to stroll along the thin sandbank that runs parallel to the reeds and beach grass on land. I nervously glance at the water either side of us - a lagoon to the right, open sea to the left.

'Is this safe?' I ask. Even though the beach is the width of a motorway, it feels like I'm walking on a tightrope.

'Most of the time,' says Chloe. 'The year before I was born a massive hurricane ripped the beach in two, pretty much where we're standing now. Even these days, parts of it get washed away. Sometimes it gets like quicksand. I think we're okay today, though they said on TV there might be a storm coming next week.' She grins.

I sense she's playing on my fear.

'After a really big storm, people find all kinds of things uncovered here. They found hundreds of old bottles once.' She turns and smiles. 'No messages though.'

My stomach tightens even more as I'm reminded of Dee's poem, and the conversation with Gloria this morning. I consider asking Chloe outright about the diary, but I don't want to alert her in case she destroys it. Perhaps she already has? I can't imagine what it could possibly contain. What might Chloe have written that somehow led to Dee committing suicide, or worse still, being murdered?

'You're lucky to see the sandbank,' says Chloe, taring me from my thoughts. 'Bill reckons it'll be all underwater in ten years or so... rising sea levels... global warming... all that stuff.'

I gaze ahead at the sandy strip that cuts through the ocean until it's out of sight. 'How far does it go?'

'Two and a half miles. On a good day, you can walk all the way to The Vineyard.'

'And is today a good day?'

'We're hanging out together, so yes, today is a really good day.'

Chapter Twenty-Nine

Bill

Bill rarely goes into Chloe's room. Her messiness irritates him. *How can anybody live in such disarray?* he thinks as he quietly closes the door behind him. Today however, is an exception. He feels he has no choice. A matter of life or death, some might say, now that their annoying Irish guest has stirred up trouble. And if he doesn't find it and someone else does, that's it. Game set and match.

He knows Chloe still has it, despite her telling him that she set fire to it and destroyed it forever. She forgets he always knows when she's lying, that's one of the advantages of the 41-year age gap between them.

She's young, but a smart cookie, so wherever she's hidden it, Bill knows it won't be obvious. In fact, he's aware there's a high probability that she wouldn't keep it in her bedroom at all. But in his mind, he needs to rule out the obvious before he looks elsewhere.

He checks every dark recess in the back of her walk-in closet, slides his hand underneath her mattress, searches her dressing table, and feels behind the books on her bookshelf.

There's one place he leaves till last, but he knows deep down it won't be there. That doesn't stop him looking. He lifts out the lace and cotton underwear, inspecting each one. As he replaces them carefully, he touches something solid tucked at the back of the drawer, a plastic container. Opening the lid, Bill sees it's more than half empty. What's left looks like some kind of health food, seeds or nuts or something, probably the latest feeding fad that Chloe has been suckered into. As he goes to put them back, one word on the label catches his eye – *avicide*, otherwise known as bird poison.

Chapter Thirty
Lyra

The beach seems to narrow even further as Chloe and I walk on. I glance back to check if we've not suddenly become cut off by a rising tide. Thankfully we haven't. Yet. We're a long way from where we started though, perhaps half a mile now. I need to take my mind off the possibility of being stranded or sucked into the sand.

'Did your mammy like to swim?'

Chloe winces and I realise what I've said.

'I'm so sorry, Chloe. I totally forgot.' Christ, what an absolute eejit!

'She couldn't swim,' says Chloe, which of course I already knew. Lord, I really am a different kind of special! 'She'd paddle a little, but she was terrified of the rip tides.'

For God's sake! Rip tides, quicksand, disappearing beaches. This place is a fucking death trap!

'Wanna swim?' asks Chloe, already taking off her sundress before I can answer. She flings it to the ground and runs into the water in her underwear. 'Come on,' she shouts. 'It's amazing.'

I don't know how she's got this hold over me, but despite my certainty that I'm going to drown, I find myself sat on the sand, peeling off my denim shorts and neatly folding my black 'Never Trust the Living' tee-shirt. *How apt is that logo?* I muse, as I stand self-consciously at the edge of the surf.

'Are you a scaredy-cat?' mocks Chloe.

'Is it safe?'

'Stop asking if everything's safe. Live a little, Lyra.' She dives under the surface. And stays there.

Shit, shit. Come on Chloe, where are you? A real fear that she's drowned takes hold and, ignoring the shock of cold water, I quickly wade in towards where she disappeared. Even though I'm only thigh-deep, I'm taken aback at the strength of the waves. They're not big, but they're relentless, urging me deeper and deeper. Chloe suddenly pops up twenty yards to my right.

'You're in! Hallelujah.' She laughs.

I try to wade towards her but I can't get closer. As soon as I stop paddling the sea pulls me further out until I can only just feel the sand under my tiptoes. 'Chloe! It's pulling me out.'

Chloe carries on laughing.

'I'm not joking. Chloe. Please, I can't get back...'

'Then come further in!'

Panic sets in as I realise I can no longer touch the bottom. 'Chloe, seriously... think I'm in one of those currents... help me...' I can feel I'm on the verge of screaming, and Chloe isn't taking me seriously.

'Chloe!' I cry one more time. This time she wades a little closer then stops.

'Let it take you out,' she shouts.

'Whaaat! No!'

'Trust me. Go with the flow. Don't fight it. When it stops, swim to the side.'

To let myself be carried out to sea goes against every natural instinct in my body. But despite my survival instinct telling me otherwise, I stop battling against it. What if she's lying? What if I just keep being swept out until I can no longer see land. I wonder how deep the water is now I'm some twenty metres from the shore. What if there are sharks circling underneath me? I think of the film, *Jaws*. Oh my God. Jaws was filmed here! Then as soon as it grabbed me, the sea let's go and I'm no longer being pushed further out. Chloe is waving her arm frantically like those men directing planes you see on airport runways. I do as she says and swim to the side. My arms and legs are heavy, but I manage to swim the ten or so metres to her. She grabs my hand and tows me to the beach.

I fall to my knees on the sand, my body trembling. My mind wants to cry but my eyes don't let me. 'I… I nearly drowned then,' I splutter, the realisation of how close to death I was fully sinking in. I now know of the terror Dee must have felt. Why the hell would anybody choose drowning as a form of suicide!

'I saved you,' Chloe says, over and over. 'I saved you.'

I take off towards the main house, leaving Chloe scrambling behind. 'Why are you so pissed at me? I saved your life!'

I swivel around, a tight ball of tension in my gut. The truth is I don't know whether Chloe saved me or purposely watched me struggle. Jackson's words come back to me. *She loves a drama.*

'You knew I couldn't swim well. Why did you suggest we go in?'

She looks genuinely taken aback. 'Did you think you might die?'

'Err, yes!'

'Was it really terrifying?'

'Yes!'

Suddenly, everything goes dead in Chloe's eyes. 'Poor mom.'

Before I can utter another word, she's darted past me in floods of tears, leaving me stood like a drowned rat and wondering if I've just been a subject in some sort of warped experiment.

Chapter Thirty-One
Lyra

After defrosting in a steaming-hot bath, I change into a pair of ripped jeans, throw on a Nirvana hoodie and head over to the main house for dinner.

Bill is sat on the porch in a wicker chair, reading *Reagan's America*. No surprises there. Spotting me, he places the book face down on his lap and stares as I take the half-dozen steps up to the house. I make a face at him, a greeting of sorts, though I'm certain he must detect that I can't abide him.

I'm surprised when he gestures to the adjacent chair. 'If you have a moment.'

I sit down, expecting him to start talking but he just stares at me like some creepy oil painting. I crack my knuckles out of awkwardness, which thankfully encourages him to speak.

'You'll get arthritis you know.'

I shrug. 'Is there something you wanted to speak to me about?'

He takes a deep breath, his brows meeting as he frowns, though his forehead remains smooth. 'Lyra, did Marie ever mention our previous housekeeper to you?'

I swallow hard. *Shit.* Has he spoken to Gloria? 'No. I don't think so.'

He studies me, gauging whether I'm telling the truth.

'Why do you ask?'

'Nothing. It's not important.'

I wait for him to elaborate but he doesn't. I want to push him on the issue, but I doubt he'd give me anything of substance, so I don't bother. 'Where's Chloe?' I ask, wondering if she's calmed down after her outburst at the beach. Did she really orchestrate the whole thing to gain insight into her mother's final moments? Surely nobody could be that sick.

'In her room,' answers Bill. 'Would you go upstairs and tell her dinner will be ready at eight-thirty? Tell her I'm making her favourite.'

My eyebrows nearly ping off my face. 'You're cooking?'

'Well, Marie is sick and I'm not totally inept, you know.' He smiles, which in itself is an oddity. 'I cooked for Dee plenty when she was... you know...' He looks away. 'She loved my spaghetti and meatballs.'

I'd almost feel sorry for him if he wasn't a complete arsehole.

'So, what *is* Chloe's favourite dish?' I ask, attempting small talk. 'What delicacy are we in store for tonight, Chef Warren?' *Chef Warren, seriously?*

'Lobster.'

'Nice. Not easy to cook though, I imagine.'

Bill smirks in a way that barely shows his teeth. 'I can show you if you like? Do you want to hear how they scream when you drop them in to boil?'

I shift in my seat as he holds my gaze a lot longer than feels comfortable.

Chapter Thirty-Two
Lyra

Sick bastard, I think as I get up to go and tell Chloe about dinner. No way am I watching a lobster be boiled alive, let alone eating its corpse. It's something I've always gone out of my way to avoid in the restaurants back in Galway. Call me a hypocrite… I love *eating* seafood but that doesn't mean I can stomach watching it die!

I make my way through the lounge, which is the equivalent of walking from Cork to Leitrim. The first thing I notice as I reach the staircase is that it's covered in blood. The second thing I see is Chloe lying unconscious.

Holy fuck! I rush over to her, Bill's name splintering the air like glass shards. 'Bill! Help! Quick!'

Underneath Chloe's head is a pool of bright red blood, matted into long, blonde hair. I shake her hard. 'Chloe!' My hand slaps her cheek. 'Jesus, Chloe, wake up!'

From behind, I hear bare feet slapping on marble. 'What's happened?' shouts Bill. 'Lyra, what have you done?'

I haul Chloe up and cradle her in my arms. I shouldn't be moving her. What if she's broken her back? 'Call an ambulance!' I look over my shoulder to Bill who is already on the phone.

'Ambulance please,' he shouts at the operator. 'My stepdaughter, she's...'

A slight movement snaps me back to Chloe who, still cradled in my arms, is now grinning at me.

She sits up. Her blood-clotted hair swings like a mane as she explodes in a fit of giggles. 'Got ya!'

I push her off me and back away, stumbling over my feet as I try to get away. 'What, you, why...?' I can only stutter random words. Her white, satin nightie is coated in blood, though I realise now it's likely food colouring or some other red condiment. What the feck has just happened?

Within seconds, Bill has barged past me and hauled Chloe to her feet. He pins her up against the wall. 'What the hell?' A vein in his forehead pulsates as he applies more pressure. 'Are you sick, child?'

I look down at his mobile on the floor, the operator still talking, then back to Chloe and Bill. He's choking her, his knuckles white around her throat.

Chloe looks at me, her eyes flashing panic. 'Lyra, help me,' she mouths.

'Get off her.' My voice is no more than a whimper.

When Bill ignores me, I pick up the phone and garble to the person on the other end, but I don't know what I'm saying.

Bill turns to me. 'Hang up. Now!'

What happens next appears as snatches of images. I drop the phone and pound Bill with my fists; his fingernails sink into my wrists. Everything turns black.

'Lyra? Wake up!'

Chloe is leaning over me. 'It's okay, he's gone now.' Her soft fingers stroke my hair. 'The cops have taken him. He can't hurt us anymore.'

I black out and when I wake again, Chloe has morphed into a paramedic. 'Don't panic,' he says. 'You've had a little fall, that's all.'

A fall? How? I sit up to a rush of nauseating dizziness. Shit! The pain is brutal. Why does my head feel as though it's been caved in with a sledgehammer?

The paramedic holds me steady. 'Just sit still, I need to check you over.'

'No!' I haul myself up, ignoring protests that I'm concussed, and immediately battle a second wave of sickness. I scan the landing and stairs. 'Where's Chloe?' Although my memory is vague, I have a blurred recollection of her being hurt. 'What happened to her?'

'She's in her room.' The sound of Bill's voice jolts a memory; Chloe was sprawled out at the bottom of the stairs, bleeding. Though she wasn't really, was she? It was a trick, a sick game, though the staircase and landing are now spotless. Did Bill clean it up?

'Lyra tried to help while I was restraining my step-daughter... for her own safety,' says Bill calmly. 'She was having a tantrum.' I look over my shoulder and see him seated in the lounge with a female police officer.

'Chloe lashed out, banged Lyra's head against the wall,' he continues. 'I will of course pay any medical bills if our guest feels she needs further treatment.' Bill throws me a look which says, *don't even think about it.*

'I *should* call an ambulance. It's a head injury,' the paramedic directs at me. 'I'm just an EMS first responder.'

'You don't need to. I'm grand, honestly, just a bit dazed.'

The paramedic isn't convinced, judging by his frown, either that or he doesn't understand my accent.

'I'm sure she'll be fine,' states Bill. 'We'll take good care of her. I'll call a nurse to come and sit with her this evening.'

'Does that sound okay to you, miss?' The paramedic is a big

fella, the muscles on his arms straining his shirt, and yet he appears to shrink in Bill's presence. I remember that Bill has the whole of the vineyard in his pocket.

'I really ought to get you checked out with a head injury and all,' says the paramedic, looking at Bill. 'But if mister Warren would prefer you to...'

'Yes, I just need to lie down, that's all.' Spending a night in Martha's Vineyard Hospital is all I *feckin* need; besides, it doesn't seem as though I have a choice in the matter. 'But...' I glance over at the officer, debating whether to ask to speak with her privately. If I make a statement that Bill was harming Chloe, he'll likely refute it, and I've already shown my memory to be hazy. In truth I'm not even certain he *was* hurting her intentionally. She was wild and deranged. Was Bill simply restraining her like he said and I got caught up in it?

'So, as Lyra doesn't want to press charges against Chloe, I think that's all,' says Bill, gesturing towards the front-door.

'Lyra? You don't want to press charges, no?' The officer shakes her head at me, a subtle, perhaps subconscious gesture, but I get the impression she doesn't want to upset Bill. 'Are you satisfied it was an accident?'

I nod, dumbly. My priority is checking to see that Chloe is okay. Despite her sick prank, I still can't help but feel protective of her.

Bill offers to see the officer and paramedic to their vehicles. A moment later, faint laughter trickles through from the hallway accompanied by Bill's assurances about the upcoming charity function. 'Please come, as my guests,' he says. Jesus, the guy has more moles than a burrow.

'I think you need a lie down.' I'm startled by Bill's sudden appearance. 'Don't bother Chloe tonight please,' he continues. 'She's fragile, needs to rest.'

'But...' I look up at him, confused. 'What happened?'

'You know what happened, Lyra.' Bill speaks so quietly I strain to hear him. 'You didn't listen. You got involved in matters you shouldn't have.'

Chapter Thirty-Three
Chloe

Chloe rests her head on the soft fur. The warmth on her cheek is comforting in the morning chill. The feel of the grey velvet carries her back to her mom's bedroom where, as a young girl she'd climb in bed and place her head on the silky smoothness of her mom's breasts during their Sunday morning snuggles.

It was a time of simplicity and freedom, the day theirs to plan. Her mom would stroke her hair while Chloe's fingers drew love hearts on her mom's belly, over and over. Nothing since that has ever come close to matching those soft, sleepy moments of security. In her mind, she has no doubt that nothing will, ever again. But for now, the feel of her face on this dead seal pup is close.

Do seals dream? she wonders through half-closed eyes as she watches the ocean froth over the golden sands of Wasque Beach. With all her heart she hopes they do. She hopes they can dream, imagine... and remember. She wants to know that they can carry good memories with them forever, a go-to place in their minds for the times when they're alone in the blind depths of darkness knowing that sharks are never far away. She feels her heartbeat quicken as she wonders whether this pup has already lived through such terror. Did it call out for its mom as the sharks circled? Did its mom come? Or was she gone forever, just like her own?

As quickly as her mood has darkened, as if by a switch, it brightens once more as she's taken back to her mom by the whisper of sand brushing through grass in the gentle breaths of ocean breeze. As she listens, her finger draws hearts on the seal and she begins to quietly sing; '*Hush little baby don't say a word, Mama's gonna buy you a mockingbird...*'

A tear rolls slowly across the bridge of her nose and onto the seal's back. Then another. And another, until a rivulet forms in the flubber and folds around its neck. The single stream crosses a crust of petrified crimson that once flowed from the corners of its coal-black eyes. She wonders if her own tears are of sadness, or of joy? She can't tell. In those quiet moments out of sight, away from Bill, Lyra, Jackson and Marie, her tears always come, they have to. And *they* never know.

When her emotion rises to the surface it has no name, but it demands to be expressed, regardless. Whatever it is that threatens to explode inside her *has* to come out in some way, so she smiles and calls it happiness. It's what they, *and* Chloe prefer. At least that way she can avoid sympathy. What that could release terrifies her.

She knows she was blessed with her mom's awesome imagination, and with that gift she knows that as long as she can smile on the outside and hide in her dreams and memories within, although the sharks are always there, waiting in the dark, she's able to at least keep them at arm's length.

The dune grass whispers again, only this time it's a warning. Feet and legs swatting away the knee-length reeds. 'There you are,' says a voice. 'I was hoping we could chat about last night.'

'Hi Lyra,' Chloe replies, emotionless and without lifting her face off the seal. 'Let's just forget about yesterday.'

'What the feck is *that*?'

Although Chloe still has her back to Lyra, it's obvious she's talking about the pup.

'A seal. Isn't it beautiful?'

'Is it... dead?' asks Lyra.

'It is,' Chloe replies sadly.

There's a silence while Lyra tries to take it all in. 'Should you be lying on it?' she asks. 'It might have... I dunno, mange or something.'

Chloe lets go of the seal, wearily sits up and squints in the morning sun. She's irritated that Lyra has disturbed the moment, but she tries not to show it. 'What's up?'

Lyra kneels beside Chloe and tentatively touches the seal with her fingertips. 'What's that on its back?' she asks, pointing to a long line of yellow and pink circles.

'Daisies.'

Lyra knits her eyebrows.

'I painted them.'

Lyra offers no response.

'Looks pretty, don't you think?'

Still nothing from Lyra.

'It's a gift. From me to the seal pup. To take on its journey home.'

Lyra's lips part, like she wants to say something but can't. Finally, she speaks.

'And that blood... around its eyes and mouth?'

The question confuses Chloe. *Why is she not impressed with the flowers?* she wonders.

'How did it die?' asks Lyra.

Chloe points to the baseball bat part-hidden in the grass beside her. '*I* killed it.'

Chapter Thirty-Four

Lyra

'It looks like it's been graffitied!' Marie's expression shifts from confusion to repulsion as she stares at the seal. 'Who in the Lord's name would do such a thing?'

I don't answer. In truth, I've barely uttered a word since this morning when Chloe admitted she'd bashed its brains in with a baseball bat. She scarpered shortly after, shouting something over her shoulder about circling sharks while I dry-retched into an empty can of pink emulsion.

'We should call the police,' says Marie firmly. 'Whoever did this is sick...'

'It was Chloe.'

A broken sound, not far from a cry, escapes Marie's lips. 'Are you sure?'

'She told me. Killed it with a baseball bat. And decorated it,' I add as an afterthought. 'Painted daisies all over it so it'd look cute in heaven.' I know I sound emotionless but I'm still numb with shock. I'm yet to get my head around last night's 'prank' let alone this. It's as if she's gone from zany to bat-shit-crazy in the blink of an eye.

Marie squeezes her eyes shut and when she opens them again,

the disbelief has been replaced with horror. 'Good God. The poor thing.'

Bending down, she whispers what I think is a prayer into the seal's ear, or where I imagine the ear would be.

'We need to phone Bill,' I urge. 'Make him come home from work. She needs serious psychiatric help.'

Marie looks up at me and I see the conflicting emotions playing out on her face. 'Bill won't agree to that. He'll brush it under the carpet like everything else, say Chloe's just upset over her mother, is acting out. He'll not want shrinks involved; I promise you.'

I know she's right. He did exactly that last night, so why should the introduction of a bludgeoned seal be any different? 'Well, we have to do something.' The frustration in my voice is masking a deep fear. Chloe is clearly unwell, and I know all too well what untreated mental illness can do to a person. 'And...' I stare back down at the seal. 'What are we going to do with that? We can't just leave it here.'

'The tide will take it,' says Marie, now stroking its back.

'If Bill doesn't step in, we go to the police,' I say, determined. 'We'll just tell them all we know, and they'll have to sort it.'

Marie stands and rakes her fingers through her hair. 'What if they lock her up? I'm certain...' she waves her hand over the lifeless lump of multicoloured flesh. 'Well, I'm sure this is a criminal offense.'

I position myself so we're eye-to-eye. 'We have to tell them everything, Marie. We give them Dee's poem and tell them about Gloria and explain about Chloe's declining mental health. We tell them all our suspicions and get them to find the suicide note.'

'Ok, *mi bonita*,' says Marie, crossing herself. 'But I have a very bad feeling about this.'

Chapter Thirty-Five
Chloe

Chloe steps from behind the tree and watches her shadow wave to Marie and Lyra.

Bye-bye friends, bye-bye.

She's epic at hide-and-seek, even Bill says so, though Bill *always* finds her.

Her shadow vanishes as bruised clouds claim the sky. She wanders to the beach house, both heart and mind buzzing in a synergy of anticipation.

So, Lyra has the poem does she? What a liar.

The beach house is unlocked and Chloe steps inside. She giggles, the shrieky sound reminding her of the hummingbird wind chime she made in first grade. As she takes the stairs, her snicker becomes a snigger.

In the bedroom, Chloe gets to work, flipping the mattress and pulling out the drawers. She chants a poem, the words forming in the dark transcendental space between mind and soul. 'The hummingbird sings a tiny trill, the smallest of birds, though blessed with skill. But once trapped, they chirp so shrill.'

A smile curls Chloe's lips as she holds up the wine bottle.

'For the caged bird,' she whispers softly into the neck, 'Now must kill.'

Chapter Thirty-Six
Lyra

'So, what do we do if Chloe's there?' asks Marie as we approach the main house. 'Do I tell her I've seen her... creation?'

'Best not. We don't know her mindset. We'll just call the police straight away.' Despite my outer coolness, inwardly I'm shitting a brick. I have no real idea if the police will take us seriously, and if they don't, we'll have lit the fuse to one mighty explosion.

'I promise you, I don't need this stress at my age, Lyra.'

I place my hand on Marie's shoulder and fight the discomfort it yields. 'I appreciate it's much harder for you than it is for me.'

'It's my life.' She looks me in the eye, worry etched in and around her dark eyes. 'I'll do the right thing, but I have to be sure what that is. If we go to the cops now, we could make the situation a million times worse. Please let's give it a little more thought. Try and find the suicide note perhaps. If the writing doesn't match then we know for sure Dee didn't write it.'

'Ok, I'll try and find Chloe and see if she knows where it is. You go into the house and act normal.'

Marie makes a face. 'How do I do that?'

'Simple. Clean it.'

Once in the house, I send Marie in search of her mop bucket while I hunt for Chloe in the downstairs rooms. Where the bejesus has she gone? I shout her name several times but to no avail, so I make my way upstairs. 'Chloe, you up here?'

Like the rest of the house, the upper floor is stylishly decorated, with heavy framed paintings, and ceramic figurines exhibited on marble pedestals. Chloe's bedroom is easy to locate courtesy of the handmade door placard bejewelled in diamantes and glitter. I'm surprised Bill has allowed something so tacky to be on display in his *House Beautiful* home. Tapping the door, I lightly call Chloe's name. There's no response, so I nudge it open and peer inside.

Aside from the unslept-in bed - probably because Chloe spent the entire night butchering marine life - the rest of the room is what mammy would have referred to as a 'holy show,' with clothes strewn across the floor and half-empty glasses littering the nightstand.

A thought strikes me. Now is my chance to find the diary.

Quickly I heave up Chloe's mattress and feel underneath but it's clear. I open a few drawers, but the neatly folded tee-shirts and shorts are a sure giveaway that Marie has been here recently. The wardrobe is just as orderly, and I can't think where else to look.

Damn.

I'm not altogether surprised. Chloe is too shrewd to leave it somewhere obvious.

Leaving this room, I continue down the hallway, intermittently stopping to have a gander in the other half-dozen rooms.

Jackson's bedroom door has been left open and, in a stark contrast to Chloe's, is a showcase of orderliness. I find myself leafing through a *Stereophile* magazine on his bedside table and then flicking through a jotter where he's scrawled down what looks like an attempt at song lyrics.

I'm drowning,
Choking on the lie,
That deep inside I cannot hide,
Screaming out, wanna fight,
But I'm dying inside.

Christ! Quickly I snap an image of it on my phone and then leaf through the rest of the pages but there's nothing much of substance; a few doodles and a list of what I take to be his favourite songs. I spot his laptop on an orderly desk and, before I have time to consider what I'm doing, I'm gawking at a screensaver of Jackson surfing. His sculpted abs and long, tanned legs make me feel things I haven't in a long while. *Jesus, get a grip, Lyra.*

Obviously, the laptop is password protected. My fingers hover over the keypad, thinking. What would Jackson use as a password? His favourite band? I type in *Stone Horses* but the screen remains locked. I try adding 123, as I know that most people combine words with numbers but that doesn't work either. If I'm not careful I'll lock him out. *Think, think.* My eyes scan the room, resting on a poster of the *Boston Celtics*. I try that, but nothing. Over on the windowsill are several framed photographs; Jackson smiling in a club with a fancy cocktail in hand, another with his arm slung around a pretty girl at the beach – his girlfriend?

Then I see it – Jackson's mother and who I assume to be him as a new-born in a hospital bed. I pick up the photo and bring it close to my face. His mum looks knackered but happy. Under the photo is scrawled writing – *Jackson and mommy – November 1993.* A lump wedges in my throat. How could any mother walk away from her baby?

Back at the laptop, I try what I know will be the final shot before I admit defeat. What did Jackson say his mother was called? Whitney? I type in *Whitney1993* and can't believe my luck when the screen unlocks.

Jesus! What am I going to do now? Find evidence I guess, but of what? Jackson visited Gloria before she went into hiding so he must be in on it, what *it* is. I scan the numerous apps on his home screen and eventually settle on Insta. There's a reel of posts about bands, soccer, and a bunch more photos of Jackson in numerous clubs surrounded by other silver spooned socialites. Facebook is useless as he hasn't posted anything for over a year and Twitter contains nothing but tons of retweets bashing Donald Trump and the occasional plug for Bitcoin. Why am I even looking at this stuff? Jackson's hardly going to have tweeted about his dad killing his stepmother, is he?

Perhaps his documents will yield more of a result. In OneDrive, I run my finger down the list of folders, settling on *Island Rentals*, one of Bill's companies that I remember Jackson telling me he managed. I'm not altogether surprised to see Gloria's name is included in the list of property tenants and a subfolder discloses that her cottage costs over a thousand dollars per month. There's just no way Gloria could afford that, so it begs the question; why is Bill allowing her to stay there rent free?

Next, I open Jackson's photo gallery and trawl through his albums. He's a keen photographer as there are numerous professional looking shots, everything from close-ups of Bill's, now deceased, bird collection to landscapes of beaches and city skylines. One folder, titled *Mom*, has been password protected which is odd. Why would Jackson want extra security on this album? I try the same password as his lockscreen and am surprised when it opens. Christ, what sort of eejit uses the same password for everything?

I swipe through numerous photos of Jackson's mom. It's clear from the quality that each photo has been scanned from an original polaroid. Like Dee, Whitney appeared to be free-spirited in her younger years, but whereas Dee was more Bohemian in style, Whitney rocked the surf-chick look with cut off denim shorts and bright cropped tops. There's a striking resemblance to Jackson. In fact, I see little likeness between Jackson and his dad which is likely why I find him hot.

Interestingly there are no photos of Bill and Whitney's wedding day. There are numerous pictures of Whitney with Jackson as a new-born, and it strikes me the difference in her appearance. Her hair is much shorter and styled neatly into a bob. Despite her olive skin, she appears washed out and is wearing frumpy dresses and jumpers, all in neutral shades of cream and brown. What does Bill do to these women? It's as though he fades them until they vanish completely; vanish being the operative word - it hasn't gone unnoticed that both of Bill Warren's wives 'vanished,' both figuratively and literally.

Surely that has to be more than a coincidence.

I swipe on, expecting to see another photo of Whitney and Jackson, so I'm shocked when a naked woman appears on screen.

My mouth falls open when I realise it's Dee.

Chapter Thirty-Seven
Marie

Marie turns and drops the mop and bucket, startled by Jackson blocking her way. 'Goodness! How do you do that?'

The bucket rolls to a stop at Jackson's feet. They both glance down at it.

'Do what?' he asks.

Marie expects him to pick it up and hand it back. He doesn't.

'Suddenly appear, without a sound?' she says retrieving it from his feet. She realises it sounds more like an accusation than an observation, but if there's one thing she hates, it's being taken by surprise.

Jackson rolls his eyes and shakes his head dismissively. It's a gesture that Marie has seen many times from his father, a mixture of arrogance and contempt.

'Have you seen Chloe anywhere?' she asks.

Jackson shrugs. 'Why?'

Marie toys with telling him about his sister and the seal but decides against it. The less he knows, the better, she thinks. 'No reason, just wondered.' She feels Jackson's eyes follow her as she walks past and up the stairs to clean Chloe's room.

She knows Jackson is hiding something, though what, she couldn't say. Does he know what happened to Dee? Clearly he knows why Gloria left so suddenly as he was the one who visited her. Perhaps Jackson's the one bribing her, but she can't imagine for the life of her why.

Chapter Thirty-Eight
Lyra

I really ought to avert my eyes. Why the bejesus has Jackson got a naked photograph of his stepmother? And why has he hidden it in a folder titled 'Mom'? I laugh, despite knowing this isn't funny. Just when I thought this family couldn't get any weirder, bang – up pops Dee Warren; wife, mother, and upstanding member of the community, posing for the camera with her hooha out, and nipples so stiff they could whip a donkey! Christ. Is *this* the secret Chloe spoke about? Did Jackson have a thing for his stepmother? Or for the love of God... were they having an affair?

It doesn't take long for me to join the dots. If Jackson and Dee were having an affair, and Chloe found out and wrote about it in her diary, and then Bill found the diary... though if that scenario was true, I'm certain Jackson would be dead too.

Unless of course Jackson needed to silence his stepmother?

A creaking floorboard is followed by footsteps on the landing, and then the sound of Jackson clearing his throat. *Shit!* I slam the laptop shut and scan the room for a hiding place. I'm sure if this was a movie there'd be a space under the bed where I could army-crawl to safety, but of course it has a solid base. The wardrobe? I yank it open, but it's stuffed to the brim with musical equipment and other electronic gadgets.

The footsteps draw closer. Christ, he's heading for the bedroom. My heart hammers so hard I feel it pulsate in my temples. I crouch down beside a large chest of drawers and catch a glimpse of Jackson's Air Jordan's crossing the room. He plonks himself down on the bed and taps away on his mobile while humming a tune – *And I love her*, by Kurt Cobain, I think, or is it *She Only Lies?* God, why am I even debating song titles right now?

A mobile rings. For a split second I fear it's mine. Then Jackson answers it. I can't make out the voice on the other end of the line but I'm certain it's male. After a brief pause, he sighs heavily, exclaims 'this is all we need,' then stands up and stomps out of the room.

I wait until I hear him taking the stairs before quickly opening up the laptop and closing the gallery. It's only as I leave the bedroom that I realise I ought to have taken a snap on my phone; but I don't suppose it matters – that image of Dee, stark bollock naked, will be forever burned into my brain.

Chapter Thirty-Nine
Marie

Marie pushes open the door to Chloe's room. As usual, it's a mess. Whereas it's obvious Lyra cleans her room before Marie can get to it, she suspects that Chloe deliberately makes it even untidier. It might be the most desired housekeeping job on The Vineyard, but it's probably also the most demanding.

She takes a second, and steps in. As she does, Jackson storms past the open doorway.

'All okay Jax...' she begins, but he doesn't acknowledge her. She shakes her head and gets to work.

She puts the mop and bucket down in the far corner, and as she does, she hears a creak underfoot. Marie knows this house from top to bottom, inside out, and none of the polished floorboards throughout have ever creaked before, everything fitted to perfection. It's Bill's way.

She tests the board again with the toe of her Reeboks. It's definitely loose. She makes a mental note to tell the maintenance man tomorrow and starts to pick up Chloe's discarded clothes. Out of the corner of her eye she sees Lyra flash by the doorway.

'*Hola, mi amor,*' she says. Her half-smile disappears when Lyra also doesn't stop to reply. *You too, now?* It's a reminder of just how insignificant she feels in this household, *but a job is a job*, she sighs. Chloe's clothes are everywhere, apart from in the wardrobe and drawers, of course. As she gathers them the floorboard won't leave her mind. Suddenly, she remembers Gloria's words, *you need to find Chloe's diary*. Is it possible that the diary is under the floorboard?

Marie looks over her shoulder at the bedroom door, puts the pile of clothes on the bed, then kneels and tries the floorboard with her hand. It lifts easily, like it's deliberately been...

'Put that back,' booms a voice from behind.

Marie stands and spins around. The look on Bill's face is an expression she's never seen before. 'I... it's loose. I was just trying to fix it.'

Marie can feel Bill's eyes boring into her. 'Get out,' he says firmly but quietly.

'But... Chloe's room... I've not...'

'Get out of this house.' His voice is low but forceful.

Marie can see the tension in his jaw. Tears fill her eyes.

Bill stands to one side and pulls the door open wider. 'You're to leave immediately, and never come back. Do you understand?'

Chapter Forty

Lyra

I slam the beach house door and lean back against it, trying to slow my breathing and attempting to make sense of what I've just seen. *What the fuck? I mean what the fucking fuck?* Jesus, this family is not for real! Sod Dee Warren, by the looks of things she was just as loopy as the rest. I need to pack my bags and get the hell out of here. Who cares if I have nowhere to go. I'll happily pitch a tent on Gratton Beach than spend another night with these loons!

I head up the stairs but abruptly stop halfway. There's laughter coming from my bedroom, a weird, childlike giggle. 'Chloe?' I shout, but there's no response. I shout louder. The laughing suddenly cuts dead. *Is it Chloe?* I can't tell.

I curl my fingers around a marble bookend as I inch along the landing. Lifting it head-height, I slowly push open the bedroom door. Chloe sits with her back to me, cross-legged in the middle of the floor. My stomach knots as I notice Dee's bottle by her side. *Shit. She found it.*

She twists her neck and smiles at me. In one hand is a pen, in the other, the poem. Chloe's arms are covered in black inky patterns, daisies, just like on the seal. 'Here it is, Lyra,' she says, cheerily. Her voice is strange, distant. 'I found it. Look.' She holds up the poem. 'Silly you. You thought you'd left it in Ireland, didn't you?' She stands and strides towards me until our noses almost touch. Her pupils are huge, black pools of hatred invading my soul. I need to run but my legs are like lead.

'You and Mom have a secret,' she hisses. Her head drops. I figure it's Chloe play-acting rejection and hurt again. 'You didn't want to share it with me?'

'Chloe... I...' As I look down, I feel a scratching and see Chloe scrawling a daisy on my arm.

'For your next journey,' she whispers.

Chapter Forty-One

Jackson

Jackson holds open the fridge door and tilts his head. He's not surprised to hear crying, Chloe's at it almost every day, even though she thinks he doesn't know. But these aren't the sobs of a fucked-up teenager. This is a sobbing he's not heard before. He closes the fridge and heads upstairs, ears tuned into what is now the sound of his dad reprimanding someone in Chloe's bedroom.

'Marie? What's going on?'

Marie stands in front of Bill, her hands together like she's pleading. Her face is a mess, smudges of mascara below each eye. Bill stands tall, his chest out, head angled back so he gazes down his nose at her. It's the same withering look Jackson has been on the end of many times over the years.

'Are you going to tell him?' snaps his dad, glaring at Marie.

Marie turns and grabs Jackson's arm. 'Jackson, you've got to help me...'

Bill holds out Marie's handbag. 'She's been stealing.' He pulls a gold watch from the bag.

'Jackson, you know I would never do that. Tell him. Tell your father I...'

No matter what's been said between Marie and Gloria, Jackson doesn't think he can let Marie suffer like this. 'Dad, I don't think Marie would...'

Bill's eyes narrow as he turns his attention to Jackson. 'Are you calling me a liar?' he asks quietly.

It's not a calmness Jackson likes, mainly because of what usually follows. 'No... I... it's just... Marie doesn't seem to be the sort of person who'd steal.'

'I'm not,' interrupts Marie. 'You know that, Mister Warren.'

Bill ignores her. His silent fury is now directed at Jackson, his eyes scouring his son's face.

Jackson knows the one thing his dad demands from him, from everybody around him, is loyalty, and he's just crossed that line. 'Maybe you made a mistake, dad?'

Bill moves closer to Jackson. He stands over him, his frame intimidating. Jackson suddenly feels six again.

'A mistake, son?' His voice is slowly gaining volume.

Jackson knows not to look him in the eye. Instead, he fixes his eyes on his dad's Italian leather shoes. They're immaculate, as always. Everything about his dad points to perfection. He despises him for that, though he knows some of the anger is aimed at himself, for wanting to be like his dad, to have people hold that same respect... or is it fear?

Bill shoves the handbag in his son's face. '*This* is her handbag,' he says as if explaining to a toddler. The leather corner scratches Jackson's forehead. 'And *this*, is my Rolex. Look.' He pushes it into Jackson's eye. '*My* Rolex was in *her* bag. Now, what is the only logical conclusion to you, Jackson.'

That you put it there because she's too close to the truth.

'Jackson?'

'That she took it, sir.' Jackson's focus is still on the floor.

'I'm sorry. A little louder. I want our thief friend to hear this.'

Jackson lifts his head and glances at Marie, his eyes stinging with regret. 'That she took it.'

'Thank-you son. So, we're in agreement. You saw her do it with your own eyes, didn't you?'

Jackson nods.

Bill turns his attention to Marie. 'Now get out of my house before I call the cops.'

Marie looks at them both, dazed. She opens her mouth as if to speak then sweeps past Bill, shaking her head.

Bill grips Marie's arm as she passes, yanking her back. 'If you say anything to anybody about this, I will make sure you go to jail. Do you understand?'

Marie nods, and dashes out of the bedroom.

Bill waits until he's sure Marie is out of earshot. 'Like I said on the phone just now, she's been talking to Gloria. I'm sure you don't need me to tell you what will happen if Gloria starts talking, do I?'

Jackson shakes his head.

'Good. Then sort it out.' He thrusts the handbag into Jackson's chest and marches out.

'What do you mean? How?' asks Jackson.

Bill turns in the doorway. 'Do whatever you have to do. Okay? Gloria can no longer be trusted to keep quiet.'

Jackson remains holding the handbag in the middle of Chloe's room, a sick feeling in his stomach. Just when he thought the dust was beginning to settle, it's all starting again.

Chapter Forty-Two
Lyra

I yank my arm away and push Chloe back. 'You need help. There's something seriously wrong with your head.'

Chloe laughs. She picks up the poem from the floor and waves it at me. 'Seems she wanted to escape from us.' Her voice grows louder. 'But I guess in the end she had nowhere to run but to her own death.'

'I don't believe she died by suicide.' The words are out before I have chance to stop them.

Chloe stares at me, her top lip curling up in disgust. 'Say that again, but slower.'

I swallow down my fear. 'What really happened, Chloe?'

Suddenly the sad Chloe is back, her voice softer, childlike again; 'I... I really don't know, Lyra,' she whispers, shaking her head. 'It just makes me so sad to think my mom felt this way about herself. Battered and beaten.' She begins to sob, her shoulders heaving up and down as a procession of tears race down her cheeks. She holds her arms out, asking for a hug.

Shit! I can't keep up with this constant changing of moods, but on the other hand, she's just a teenage girl in need of female comfort after losing her mom. I'm not exactly the right person to provide that, but despite her… issues, shall we say, I still can't help but feel sorry for the poor girl. I know all too well how it feels to be abandoned.

'Come here,' I say, squeezing her tight. As I gently stroke her hair, I'm still tense with the uncertainty that at any moment she could switch again, do anything. I decide to try and get as much out of her as I can while she's at a weak point. 'What do you remember about your mammy just before she died,' I whisper. 'How did she seem?'

'She *was* really depressed, you know, just on a huge downer,' she says in between sniffs. 'I tried to cheer her up, I promise I did, but she'd just cry and cry. I couldn't do anything.'

'I'm sure you did your best, Chlo, I'm sure you did your best.' I realise I'm rocking her now, like an actual mother. *Jesus, what is this family doing to me?* 'And did she mention anything that was bothering her?' I'm referring to the naked image of Dee on Jackson's computer but I don't share this detail with Chloe. If she doesn't already know, the revelation could tip her over the edge completely.

Chloe is quiet for a moment, the crying subsided; 'Just the arguing with Bill, and Jackson too. I used to hear her and Jackson arguing at night sometimes, like really shouting. They hated one another.'

My stomach turns over. 'Why?'

Chloe shakes her head. 'I could never tell.'

I don't know if she means she couldn't tell why her stepbrother hated her mum and vice versa, or that Chloe could never tell me because it would be too shocking, like if she knew Dee and Jackson had slept together!

'I know mom went to the doctor,' she says, 'about the depression. She was putting on lots of weight and her moods were insane. It was me who suggested she go. Bill found out and went crazy.'

'Why?'

'He didn't want people to know his wife was depressed, obviously.' She shrugs as though it's a perfectly logical explanation. 'It was embarrassing for him. He demanded she stopped taking the medication.'

My heart beats so fast I can feel it in my temples. 'My God! He never should have forced her to stop taking her meds like that. When did he tell her to stop?'

'It was a few days before she killed herself. They had a huge row...he threw them in the trash.'

Chloe is gawking at me like she doesn't understand what the big deal is. Why isn't she making the connection?

'I need some air.'

Having made my way outside, I stand at the edge of the pool and stare into the water. The Atlantic breeze stirs tiny ripples on the surface breaking up my reflection like a cheap video effect. I look distorted. It's exactly how I feel.

Another reflection appears in the pool and snaps me out of my dark trance. It's Marie, and she's clearly distraught.

Chapter Forty-Three
Lyra

'What do you mean he's fired you? Why?'

'Not here,' shushes Marie. I follow her eyes up to the bedroom window where Chloe is waving excitedly at us. 'Should I ask why she's covered in pen marks?'

'Don't.'

Marie power walks through the gardens to the sandy path that leads to the beach. I trail behind, my brain a carousel of unanswered questions; why has Marie been sacked? Will Chloe tell Bill about the bottle? Why does Jackson have naked pictures of his stepmother on his computer and, most importantly, what the feck happened to Dee Warren? I know I have to tell Marie about the naked picture, but right now I need to find out why she's been fired.

'So, come on, spill.' Now on the beach, I look over my shoulder to make sure we haven't been followed. 'What the hell happened?'

'Bill's accused me of stealing from him.' Tears spring into Marie's eyes, though I sense from the tightness of her jaw that she's more angry than sad. 'He had hold of my bag in front of Jackson and there were valuables in there, watches, jewellery. I never stole a thing, I promise you.'

'Of course. I'd never think that for a second.' I feel a sudden urge to cry, to relieve some of the pressure that's been building inside of me since this morning when Chloe announced she'd killed that poor, innocent seal. But I know I won't, I can't. Ever since the day I found mammy dead it's as though the tears have frozen over. Instead, I ball my hands into fists, and do nothing.

'He obviously knows I'm on to him,' says Marie, her voice now laced with panic. 'He said I need to leave immediately and to stop spreading rumours or he'll go to the cops.'

I feel my breathing becoming shallower. This is all getting out of hand. 'I heard Jackson on the phone earlier. He said, *this is all I need*. He must have been talking to Bill. Do you think Gloria has been in contact?' If Bill knows we suspect Dee was murdered, it dawns on me we could be in danger too. 'But If Bill's going to these lengths,' I add, 'then he's definitely hiding something. I say we go the police, now. There's no other option.'

'No. They'll believe Bill. I'll be arrested.' Marie intertwines her fingers and holds them up to her face as if in prayer. 'Good Lord, I'll go to jail.'

'No, you won't. They won't believe Bill.'

'They will!' Her voice breaks. 'You don't know how it works here. Bill's likely got the district attorney on his payroll.'

I hate to admit it but she's likely right. *Christ!* Why did I have to come here? Why didn't I just stay in Ireland and leave Marie to her 'bad feeling' which she'd never have acted on if it wasn't for me sticking my oar in. I didn't even know Dee bloody Warren but judging by the Page Three selfie she was far from innocent; why the hell am I risking everything for a dead woman I've never met! *Because of mammy,* a little voice whispers. *Because they all told you she killed herself but you know it isn't true.*

'Okay Marie,' I say, determined that I'll do whatever it takes to nail Bill, with or without the police. 'What do you want to do?'

'I don't know. It's all such a mess.' Marie wanders over to the shore, takes off her trainers and lets the water run over her feet. As her loose coral dress billows in the wind, my heart sinks. Marie, anxious and afraid, reminds me of mammy when she was struggling with the weight of the world. She too would find solace in the sea breeze, but unfortunately it was never enough to blow away her pain.

I gaze at Marie for a while, lost in memories that sift through my mind like the sand between my toes. Just like mammy, Marie's a good person, one of life's beautiful souls and I wish with all my heart I could go up to her, take her by the hand and tell her that she's the first person since mammy died that has accepted me for me. I hate myself for not being able to comfort her properly, that the very idea of me showing any vulnerability, even with Marie, is like fingers down a chalkboard.

But Chloe? There's something about her that makes me want to break out of my comfort zone, as though by seeking justice for her mother I can for mine too. Perhaps in Chloe I've simply found a more damaged soul than mine, and somehow it's a relief.

'I'm going to walk, Lyra.' Marie turns to face me, and I see shame in her eyes. 'I'm sorry. I can't take on Bill, he's too powerful. You should get on the next flight home, *mi bonita*.'

I shake my head, an inner determination taking hold. I can't allow Bill to do this to Marie, I won't allow his money and influence to win. 'I'm going to stay. I'll figure this out, trust me. I'm not letting Bill get away with this. I'll not let him do this to you.'

Marie cups my face in her hands. 'You're a beautiful person, Lyra.' She smiles, but it doesn't quite reach her eyes. 'Listen.' She drops her voice to a whisper even though there's nobody else around. 'I found a loose floorboard in Chloe's room. I'm sure that's where the diary is. Chloe knows something, and I can guarantee it will be in that diary. Find it, and ring me when you do.'

Chapter Forty-Four
Jackson

Jackson watches from behind a redwood as Gloria carries a pitcher of lemonade and what looks like a bowl of breakfast cereal onto the porch. She pours herself a glass then shouts something to Cole sat cross-legged on the clearing in front of the house. Then she flops down onto a two-seater swing chair, still talking to her son. Jackson is too far away to hear what she says, or to hear any creaking as Gloria swings in and out of the beams of sunlight that slice through the trees.

He's engrossed in this mother and son interaction... any mother and son interaction for that matter. It always stirs a mixture of emotions. Mostly sadness, but also envy. It just doesn't seem fair that he missed out on so much while other kids get the love and attention that he so craves.

Chloe knows how to get the attention, if not the love, that's for sure. Yesterday's antics on the stairs were a prime example of that. He can't say he was that surprised when Bill told him about her pantomime. Not a lot she does surprises him anymore. But that's not the kind of attention he wants, or anyone should want. That's just attention for the sake of attention. Jackson wants genuine attention, real interest in who he is, not the forced kind.

One time, while having a breakfast burrito at E-Love after a one-nighter in Edgartown, he couldn't take his eyes off a mother and her teenage son sat at a table on the decking next to his. The mom was desperately trying to have a conversation with her son while they ate breakfast, but the little shit wouldn't look her in the eye, just ignored her as he stuffed his pimply face. Jackson remembers glaring at the boy, his eyes boring into him urging him to speak to his mother, to savour that time, that attention. And then the boy noticed Jackson staring and glowered back. 'What you staring at, asshole,' murmured the teen. He remembers the boy's mom turning beetroot red with shame and embarrassment. Jackson could have killed the boy there and then, shoved that filthy Red Sox baseball cap down the spotty youth's throat and watched him choke to death. He often wishes he had.

In the shade of the woodland, he feels that same anger rising now as Cole continues to ignore Gloria's calling. *Okay, he's still young, but doesn't he know he could lose his mom in the blink of an eye or the pull of a trigger?* Jackson knows he's close enough to be able to take them both out with two clean shots, and they'd never know a thing.

Since he was a kid, his dad had always been impressed with Jackson's shooting ability after teaching him to pick off migrating wildfowl on Pocha Pond during Fall. A couple of times the police had turned up, but when they saw whose son it was, they were quickly on their way. It made him feel proud to be a Warren. At least it did back then.

Jackson tries to think of anything else for which his dad is proud of him. He can't and focuses again on Gloria and Cole in the woodland clearing.

It's Bill's big charity event tonight and he wants everything taken care of before guests arrive. It's quite simple; paying Gloria off and settling her in a new home wasn't enough to keep her quiet. She's been talking to Marie and can't be trusted to stick to their 'arrangement' so something more drastic has to be done.

Jackson knows what he must do, though he can't be seen to be involved; besides, why would he want to when he has so many other people to turn to? He pulls out his phone and stabs in a number. He reminds the man on the other end of the line that he owes Jackson a favour and that it's now payback time.

Chapter Forty-Five
Lyra

The day has arrived. Bill's 'infamous' auction; a yearly ritual where rich folk pretend to give a damn about others less fortunate. I'm already dreading it, not least because I don't have Marie's calming presence.

Since Marie was fired yesterday, I haven't had a single opportunity to get inside of Chloe's room. She's stalked me continuously, as though she knows what I'm planning. I wouldn't be surprised if she hasn't already moved the diary. As for the suicide note, I have no clue where to even look.

In truth, I'm fed-up and contemplating jacking it all in and heading back to Ireland. Even the weather appears to be mirroring my mood; bruised clouds gather on the horizon and the sea has taken on a deathly pallor. It lies ominously still, like a patient at the end of palliative care. It's the kind of day that would normally throw me into a fit of melancholy, a day for lying in a dark room playing songs about love lost, lives taken, and hearts broken. But that's in Ireland. Here I don't have such luxuries as dark rooms and being left alone to wallow, as the bundle of energy now heading my way proves.

Chloe cracks a toothy grin. 'Lyra, I'm so super psyched for the party later, do you want to get ready together?'

I must look at her as though she's lost her mind, which surely she has. How can she act as though the last few days haven't happened? Has she seriously forgotten bludgeoning a seal, faking her death, and doodling daisies on my arm?

I place the notebook face-down on my lap and study her for a moment; she's so beautiful, angelic even, and yet there's something slightly off about her, as though she's a prototype for perfection as opposed to the real deal. 'I think I'd prefer to get ready by myself Chlo,' I say tensely, worried in case she blows her fuse again. 'I'm going to be writing pretty late and then will just throw everything on last minute.'

Chloe sticks her hands on her hips and huffs. 'You're so boring, Lyra. Parties are *all* about the prep. We have to do each other's hair, nails, makeup.'

'I just need a bit of time, Chloe, please.' I know I sound exasperated but that's exactly what I am. 'Things haven't been great recently here, have they?'

Chloe frowns, as though she hasn't the first idea what I'm talking about. 'Why?'

Why? Is this girl serious? 'Well Marie for starters,' I say, now closing the book and standing. 'Do you honestly believe she stole from Bill?'

'Well, she *was* poor?' she says, shrugging.

'That doesn't automatically make her a thief! I take a calming breath and sit on the arm of the wicker chair. I know that I can't appear to be on Marie's side if I'm going to remain at the Warrens. 'Anyway, it's not just Marie,' I say lightly. 'You've been...'

'What?'

'Well, a little off you know. The seal,' I elaborate when Chloe continues gawping at me. 'And the stunt on the stairs.'

'Oh that.' Her rosy cheeks betray her embarrassment. 'Oh, that was just a joke. A bad one, admittedly. I don't think I grasp humour very well sometimes. Least that's what Bill says. He thinks I may be on the spectrum.'

I imagine Bill's likely right, though *what* spectrum exactly? Autistic? Anti-social personality? Full-blown nutjob?

'Well, I need to get back to the keyboard,' I say, waving my notebook as evidence. 'I almost have the story idea nailed so now I need to write it.'

'Oh, I've read *Mother*, by the way,' states Chloe as I make to leave.

I raise an eyebrow. 'Thought you'd already read it?'

'Again,' she says smugly, not missing a beat. 'Now I know you. Is it semi-autobiographical?'

I nod. 'It's best to draw on personal experience in writing, or in my experience at least.'

'So did your mother really get murdered?'

The pain in my heart returns as I'm reminded of mammy. 'It's just fiction,' I reply awkwardly. 'Most is made up.'

'That's sick.' Chloe scowls at me. 'Don't think it's my head you ought to be worried about Lyra.'

She turns and walks away from me with her head held high, as though she's won a game I didn't even realise we were playing.

Chapter Forty-Six
Bill

Bill pulls Dee's jewellery box from the wall safe. He places it carefully on the dressing table and runs a finger lightly across the gilt-edged rim. There's so much substance in this one little container, he thinks; its contents holding the power to transform, to impress, to influence.

He still remembers the meticulous thought he put in to choose the right accessories for Dee to wear at a given function; a string of perfectly round, wild South Sea pearls when all the other ladies would be wearing cheaper cultured pearls; black-gold earrings set with black diamonds when other ears dangled with unimaginative plain yellow gold; and an eight-carat emerald-cut diamond ring that never failed to outshine the hands of even the most affluent of women.

He lets out a sigh. He misses those moments. For him, it was almost an artform selecting the right jewellery, something he took extremely seriously. His face reddens as he remembers Dee's usual reaction. Did she care? Not in the slightest. 'Just let me choose my own goddam necklace', she'd whine. As if she had any clue as to what worked best! Bill knew she was never appreciative of the time he put in to help her improve herself, just like his first wife, Whitney. To be honest, neither woman showed gratitude for anything he did for them. And yet deep down, they must have realised they were nothing without him, just cheap, low-life sluts with no money, no style and no class.

Good riddance to the pair of them, Bill thinks.

Chapter Forty-Seven
Lyra

Stumbling across the binoculars in the beach house seemed like fate.

Peering through them, I scan the second story of the main house until I find Bill's bedroom window. It occurs to me that if I were fictionalising his room, I'd have described it just as it is; opulent yet characterless. In the centre of the room, a huge king-sized bed is draped with crisp white linens and a fireplace is nestled in the corner surrounded by two armchairs and a small table. Like the rest of the house, expensive artwork adorns the walls, and as expected, the whole room is as neat as a pin.

Bill is searching through the contents of a box, pulling out jewellery, inspecting it and then putting it back. I can't hear what he's saying, but his lips are moving, as though muttering to himself. It's difficult to work out his mood because his face is forever stiff as a corpse thanks to Massachusetts best Botox.

He then places the box into what I think is a safe and takes out a piece of paper. Even with the binoculars it's impossible to see what's written on it but judging by Bill's smirk I know it's something I need to get my hands on. Could it be Dee's alleged suicide letter?

Folding up the note, Bill places it back inside the safe, slams the lid closed and keys in a number.

0646

Checking himself in a full-length mirror, he straightens his shoulders and heads out of the room.

A few moments later, Bill's Mercedes rolls past the beach house and out of the iron gates.

Wasting no time, I head for the main house and take the stairs. 'Chloe, Jax, you guys up here?' I shout, not wanting a repeat performance of yesterday. Dee's naked image flashes in my mind's eye. *What the hell were you playing at, woman?*

Now on the landing, I call out once more but the upper floor is so quiet I can hear myself breathing. I'm pretty sure Jax is out because I heard his Mustang leave this morning and to my knowledge he hasn't come back. I've no idea where Chloe is, that girl could just as easily be building sandcastles on the beach as fashioning tonight's outfit from whale blubber.

I come to Chloe's bedroom first and gently tap on the closed door. 'Chlo?' When there's no answer I try the handle but the room is locked. Why has she locked it? *Damn, I'm never going to get my hands on the bloody diary.*

I head down the corridor to Bill's room and lightly push open his bedroom door. The gleaming hardwood floor stops me in my tracks. If I leave so much as one footprint Bill will know I've been here. I remove my Doc Martins and place them by the door. Sucking in a shaky breath, I head straight for the safe which is built into the wall and key in the code.

Inside lies the solid gold jewellery box I saw Bill with earlier and a single scrap of paper. No wads of cash like I expected, though I suppose Bill Warren only trades with diamonds and bribes.

Carefully, I unfold the paper, making a mental note of the folds so I can put it back just so. Even before I read the words I know it's Dee's suicide note, certain that there's nowhere else Bill would keep it.

I scan the words, feeling a deep sadness wash over me. It's another poem, only this time there isn't any hidden meaning:

Vanished are the once-vibrant aspirations, the radiant yearnings, the fervent cravings
Quenched, extinguished like flames in the depths of the night.
Love, happiness, and mirth - all surrendered and forsaken,
Leaving behind a mere shadow of the woman I once was.

I am weary of this existence, this ceaseless circle of monotony,
Desperate to break free, to sense vitality and verve.
I long to let out a piercing scream, to unleash my voice,
But the grip of trepidation and uncertainty keeps me in check.

I am apologetic for the grief my demise will bring,
Yet for me, the end holds no agony nor sting.
As a mother and wife, I have stumbled and fallen short,
Thus, death remains the sole answer to life.

Folding the note, I place it back in the safe and let out a sigh of relief. Though heartbreaking, there is one thing I am certain of. The handwriting matches the poem I found in the bottle.

Which can only mean that Dee Warren really did take her own life.

Chapter Forty-Eight
Lyra

Bill's guests are arriving, and I'm not even dressed. Every Mercedes and Jaguar that pulls up to the house heightens my anxiety tenfold. So many rich people to talk to, so many confident couples to judge me. What am I supposed to say to them? - *nice to meet you, you seem posh!*

This is not my place. These are not my people. The two statements have lodged themselves in my mind and I can't shake them off. I peer from behind the curtain as another elegant couple dressed to the nines emerge from a powder-blue Bentley.

I mean look at me! You can't polish a turd. The urge to get on a plane right now and leave this crazy place is immense. But I promised Marie I'd help sort this mess out. Ok, so Dee Warren wasn't murdered but Gloria was still silenced for reasons unknown, there's still a missing diary that contains God knows what and Marie has still been framed for theft.

I start pacing. *God, what to do, what to do.*

I hurl my empty suitcase onto my bed and start chucking my clothes in.

'Lyra, what are you doing?'

'Jesus wept, you made me jump, Bill.'

Bill waggles a finger at the case and makes a questioning expression.

'Oh that. I was just sorting a few clothes out, you know, things I'm not going to wear.'

He nods, then steps fully into the room. I hadn't seen, but he's carrying two boxes, one little, one small. He passes me the bigger one. 'I know you went shopping with Chloe, but I feel tonight calls for something even more special... so I bought you this.' He puts the box on the bed, opens the lid and pulls out a pastel pink evening dress with gold trim. *He actually wants me to wear this! It looks like something from a fancy dress shop.* I try to conceal my horror with a smile that at least hints at gratitude, but my mouth has other plans and I'm sure it comes across as a grimace.

'Wow, it's... err, gorgeous.'

'I'm glad you like it,' says Bill with a proud smile. 'And these...' He opens the smaller box and takes out a pair of pearl earrings, '...will match it beautifully.' He holds the monstrosities in the palm of his hand. I immediately recognise them from some of the photos of Dee and his first wife that I found in the drawer downstairs.

The pressure of holding everything in finally overflows and before I can stop myself the words come out. 'Listen, I'm really, really grateful Bill. The dress, the earrings... they look amazing. It's just that, well... they're just not me, if you know what I mean.'

Bill exhales loudly through his nose. 'I know it's not what you're used to, but you've moved on since you got here. He pauses as he tries to find the right words. 'You've matured. This is a very different world to one that you're used to, I get that,' he continues.

You can say that again!

'But you're holding yourself back. You think you can't change, better yourself. But you can. You deserve a better life, Lyra, you really do.'

It's the most words I've heard Bill speak since I arrived, but he's not done yet.

'Let go of the past. Look at the new you, the elegant you,' he passes me the dress, 'the beautiful you.'

Maybe he's right, maybe I am stuck in my ways, afraid of change. Okay, it isn't something I'd buy myself, but it's actually a gorgeous frock. 'Okay,' I say. 'Thanks.'

He gently places the pearl drops on the bed. 'Wear the earrings too,' he says quietly and backs out of the door before suddenly leaning back in. 'And the make-up?' He draws a circle around his face; 'Take it all off, okay?' He closes his eyes and nods as if this is the final say on the matter, then quietly closes the door behind him.

Chapter Forty-Nine
Chloe

The velvet hem of Chloe's blood-red dress brushes the lawn as she sashays in front of a string quartet, their arms moving in unison as they fill the starlit night with a harmony of violins and cello. Understandably, all heads turn and follow her.

She chooses to play the part, offering up air kisses and fluttering her eyelashes at the men; they love it when she plays their games; the wives not so much, but that only adds to Chloe's amusement. Despite knowing she's a sure knock-out, Chloe's all too aware that since becoming Bill's stepdaughter, she's now a commodity as opposed to a human being. Anything that can raise the social standing of these ass-kissers, including pretending to care about her wellbeing, is fair game. In reality, the women hate her. And the guys? They probably just want to fuck her.

Chloe helps herself to a glass of champagne from one of several white-shirted waiters who float around like phantoms - seen and not heard, yet with no meaningful presence. Flute in hand, she leans against a tree that's choked in fairy lights and watches the various groups swell and dissolve. She finds the power play fascinating; it's little more than a playground, though admittedly one where all the cool kids have congregated. But with any group, there's inevitably a hierarchy and Chloe finds it an honour to witness the moment pockets of these prissy, rich arseholes realise they're worth little more than the scholarship kid they once bullied.

Sinking the champagne, Chloe goes in search of a refill. Bill wouldn't take kindly to her drinking but if she's going to get through the evening with air in her lungs, she must find a way to blot out the 'crazies'; to be 'normal' as Bill demanded.

Chloe finds the subject of normality fascinating. What is normal anyway? Playing by somebody else's rules? Climbing the social ladder like these dimwits only to reach the top and discover your inner demons beat you to it, because they can fucking fly! No, Chloe is still to figure out what normal is, only knowing what it's perceived to be. She's aware that most people can play *normal* better than she can; to most it comes easily. For her, it's a pretence she must wear for a while despite knowing it doesn't suit her – much like the dress Lyra is wearing.

Lyra is standing by the pool, looking as awkward as a transvestite with an erection.

Skulking over to Lyra and Bill, she's careful to keep herself hidden within the masses. Bill is beside Lyra and they're talking to a group of people Chloe doesn't recognise – though why would she? Women who think they're beautiful when in fact they're just rich, and men with moustaches straighter than their bow ties is par for the course. It's not so much a glitch in the Matrix than a full-blown malfunction.

Chloe's stomach flips. Bill has his hand on the small of Lyra's back and is running his ring finger down her spine. From Chloe's vantage point she's unable to see Lyra's reaction but imagines she's enjoying it. Why wouldn't she be? Bill is the king but there is no way Chloe will allow Lyra to be his queen. What a bitch, thinks Chloe. As if sucking up to Jax the jackass wasn't bad enough, now that fucking Lyra wants to muscle in on Bill! Chloe marches over and barges in-between them.

'There you are,' she says to Bill brightly. She links her arm through his, despite feeling the resistance. What's wrong with him? Chloe knows he likes to play it safe at these kinds of events, but surely, he must be keen to introduce her.

'Have you met my daughter?' Bill asks his brown-nosed hangers-on. Before they can answer, Bill turns his back on them to address Chloe. 'Have you been drinking?' He leans in, presumably to smell her breath.

'A little,' she smiles. 'It's a party, isn't it?'

Bill wags his finger at her. 'You're a child, you don't drink. Understand?'

'A child am I?' she says, crossing her arms. 'Are you sure?'

Bill grips her arm and pulls her away from the group. 'Go to your room right now.'

Chloe wants to protest but the warning in Bill's eyes is enough to keep her mute. She looks to Lyra for support, but Lyra isn't even looking at her; in fact, she thinks Lyra may have fallen out with her, though she can't imagine why.

Forever the dutiful daughter, Chloe does as instructed despite feeling twisted up inside.

It's only as she passes the beach house that a smile grows on her lips.

She'll show them that Chloe Warren is anything but a little girl!

Chapter Fifty
Lyra

Man, how this lot drone on. And the same questions, to me and each other, over and over. *How do you know Bill? Where are you from? What do you do? Blah-de-blah.* Instead of having name tags, they should all wear badges stating their net worth, then they wouldn't have to waste time with those who have nothing of value to offer.

Naturally I get short shrift when we get to question three. 'Oh, an author. How... interesting. You should write a book about me, I've got some interesting stories,' they chortle.

I'm sure you've not mister, I'm sure you've not.

And then they're off with their 'well, it's been lovely talking to you,' exit speech, and here I am again, standing about like a spare prick at a wedding. There's only one thing for it. 'Waiter!'

After three more glasses of champagne, I'm feeling a lot more at ease with the proceedings. So much so, that I invite myself to join a group of five people chatting at the bottom of the lawn. 'Hi, I'm Lyra,' I say with a short, cheery wave.

'Laura! So pleased to meet you. This is Daphne my wife, and this is Bruce and Lottie, very dear friends of mine. And this...' the man gestures to a creepy looking dude with a bald head and oversized teeth, '...is John.' He then cups his hand to his mouth and leans in as if sharing a secret. 'John just lost his wife,' he says in a stage whisper. 'CEO of an investment bank. Loves the Irish. You should speak to him.'

I ignore the attempted matchmaking, and the seedy wink. 'Nice to meet you all,' I drawl with a smile. 'And you are?' I ask the marriage broker.

'I'm sorry?'

'You introduced everyone else, but I didn't catch *your* name?'

The man looks around at the others bemused. They all give a little shrug of the shoulders and apologetic smiles.

'I'm really sorry, but I can't understand a word you're saying,' says the man. 'John? You've been to Ireland. Can you translate?'

And of course, the moment has gone, just like that. With a wet raspberry that I'm sure everyone can hear, my confidence deflates as quickly as champagne breathed air into it. I make my excuses by announcing I'm just going to the loo, but again I'm greeted with a battery of blank, staring faces.

As I walk away the alcohol kicks in even more. I realise the ground isn't as cooperative as it was, and I have to give all my focus to not falling arse-over-tit in these ridiculous heels. Leaning on the back of a garden chair, I struggle to pull the thin strap further up around my ankle and hear Bill's voice mentioned. The conversation seems to be taking place in deliberately hushed tones. I continue fiddling with my shoe as I tune in to the two couples.

'He might be a rich, good-looking bastard but all his women leave him,' says one of the two silver-haired men. 'One disappears and the other tops herself. Or so we are led to believe.'

'Bill would never do such a thing,' states one of the women.

'Don't you be fooled. He's no saint,' smirks another female. 'Ask half the women here.'

'Exactly,' says the man over the laughing, 'I'm just telling you what's doing the rounds on the mainland... that Bill Warren killed

Dee. Had defensive wounds on her by all accounts, but of course that was all hushed at the post-mortem.'

'Hearsay,' argues Bill's fangirl, obviously fancying herself as the next Mrs. Warren, though judging by her rotund figure and double chin she doesn't stand a chance. 'He's a grieving widower and you ought to be ashamed.'

'Hey, don't shoot the messenger.' The man holds his hands up in defence. 'But you know what they say. There's no smoke without fire... and with one wife dead and the other as good as - it's a raging inferno if you ask me.'

Chapter Fifty-One
Chloe

Chloe stands naked in Lyra's bedroom, staring into dark, endless eyes, a grin widening on whore's lips.

'Hello sad clown, tears upside down, a white face dripping red,' she whispers.

Emotion weaves her words, unsteady breaths providing punctuation for one of the many poems stored in her mind.

Chloe's reflection excites her. She runs cold hands over tiny breasts and cries for help despite knowing nobody will hear. They *never* hear... or rather refuse to. Her hands wander lower, the touch a burning ache. Closing her eyes, she shudders.

Coming to, Chloe smirks and flutters her lashes like butterfly wings. 'Your laughter's all lies, your costume a guise,' she says to the reflection. 'Now it's time to unmask.'

Chapter Fifty-Two

Lyra

With the conversation having now moved on to more trivial matters, I go in search of stronger alcohol.

Jackson nods as I totter towards him. *In the name of God, please don't let me fall over in front of him.* He's sat on a low wall that surrounds the pool area. A man, several years his senior, sits with him and laughs at something he said. *Are they talking about me? Is it that obvious I'm rat-arsed?*

The man stands and leaves as I approach Jackson. I stand in front of him, hoping I'm not swaying.

Jackson pats the vacated spot next to him. 'Have a seat.'

I don't know if it's because I'm looking at him through champagne goggles, but he's a real stunner tonight in his tux and dickie bow, like a junior James Bond but with a bad-ass attitude.

'You enjoying it?' I ask, determined not to slur.

He rolls his eyes and smiles. 'Rather be at a Loft gig with you.'

I feel myself melting into the wall. 'Me too.'

'Looks like you're making the most,' he says, gesturing at the half-full champagne flute in his hand. He hands it to me, and I knock it down in one.

'Thanks,' he says jokingly, as I pass it back empty.

I put my head on his shoulder, very un-Lyra like of me. *God, how much HAVE I drunk?* I let out a deep sigh as we watch the garden party continue around us. 'It's testament to the size of your garden that you can fit so many pricks in one space at the same time.'

Jackson laughs. 'And they say size doesn't matter.'

I'm loving the flirty banter. It's a side I've not seen before. I make a mental note to get Jackson pissed more often. I put my hand on his leg. He must work out. I can feel his tight thigh muscles under his black pants. This man is full of secrets! 'So, you wanna break away, go find something more interesting to do?'

'What did you have in mind?' he answers.

'I'll leave that to your imagination.' I slide my hand further up his thigh, but he grabs it and pushes it away.

'Don't,' he says quietly.

I smile up at him and try his chest, tucking two fingers into a gap between his shirt buttons.

He stands suddenly. 'I said don't.' This time he says it with real intent.

I'm genuinely flabbergasted at this sudden change. 'But... I thought... me and you...'

'Listen...' his voice is cold, annoyed. 'I'm not interested, Lyra.'

'Well, you've got a funny way of showing it.' I don't know what I feel more, offended or embarrassed. Alcohol-fuelled anger comes out instead. 'Not your type, am I, eh Jackson? Too young?'

He looks down at me, brow furrowed in confusion. 'What the fuck are you talking about?'

'Maybe you like them older... like your stepmother?'

His mouth opens, but no words come out. He just shakes his head as if he couldn't believe I would say such a thing.

'Well, is that true?' I continue.

He scowls as he leans in, his eyes burning into mine. 'You're playing a very dangerous game, Lyra,' he says menacingly, then storms off, leaving me to both regret drinking so much, and to wonder if I've just been threatened.

Chapter Fifty-Three
Lyra

I stagger after Jackson while shouting his name. He disappears into a throng of people who are spilling drinks and talking shite. I attempt to navigate my way through them, but my vision is blurred. *Christ, a single helping of the toffs was bad enough without seeing double.*

Sod it. I plonk myself down in the middle of a random group and remove my shoes; why the feck am I dressed like Columbia and Frank N Furter's love child anyway? Who am I trying to kid?

Disapproving tuts shower down on me like confetti as I struggle with the shoe clasps. This is another reason why I prefer Ireland. At least in Galway, my antics would be celebrated with a shot of Jaeger and a good old rendition of *All For Me Grog*. I fling the shoes to one side and use the tail of some old fella's jacket to pull myself up. He grins inanely as I stumble into him.

I somehow make it to the porch steps but they're rocking side-to-side like fairground fun-house stairs. *How much have I actually drunk?* I manage the first two and then crawl the rest. Holy Shit, now the clutch bag is vibrating. No, correct that, the phone in the clutch bag is vibrating. For a split-second I think it might be Tom.

A dead-weight hits my stomach as I remember his infidelity. *He was wearing socks Lyra, for Christ's sake. Forget him.*

Gradually, the caller ID comes into focus. *God, not now.* I scan the vicinity to check nobody is earwigging. 'Gloria?' There's a pause on the line. 'Gloria, is that you?'

'Lyra?' Gloria chokes out my name. 'You at the Warren's?'

'Yes.'

'I got to speak to Marie,' she garbles. 'She there?'

'Erm, no. She was fired.'

Gloria dissolves into a floor of tears. 'I need her to take Bubba. He can't see me like this. Do you know where she's at? Her phone's off.'

It's obvious from Gloria's slurring that I'm not the only one tanked up. 'I'm not sure where she lives. What do you mean you need her to take Bubba? What's happening?'

'Bill!' she shrieks. 'He's not who you think he is, he...' her words are drowned out by more sobbing.

A surge of adrenaline instantly sobers me up. 'What Is it, Gloria? What did Bill do?'

'He wants to shut me up for good, about that night, he'll stop at nothing. Jackson, he...' she suddenly screams at somebody to go back to bed. 'Bubba,' she says by way of explanation. 'He confused... he don't know what's happening. We're in this strange old place and...'

'What place? Aren't you at the cottage?'

'No. And I shouldn't be using the phone. Jackson he...'

What? Jackson what? Christ this is getting too much. Why have I been trying to sort this out myself? I should've just gone to the police the minute I suspected something untoward.

'Jackson's a good boy,' says Gloria, now sniffling. 'Not like his pa. I practically brought him up when I worked at the house. That boy was only a child when I took the job. Jackson, he'd never want to hurt me and Bubba. He had a friend take us some place safe, said we had to disappear, said it was the only way. Only

Bubba, he special, he don't understand. This all too much for him.'

My brain tries to process what Gloria is saying. Bill wanted Gloria, what? Threatened? Killed? 'You gotta go tell Jackson to come and get Bubba,' garbles Gloria. 'Tell him to take Bubba to Marie, he can't see me like this.' She gulps down a hysterical sob. 'Lyra, I ain't got long... the pills...'

Fuck! I suddenly realise that Gloria isn't drunk, she's taken an overdose. A memory wells up inside of me like a physical mass. No images, just the feeling of being sucked through a void of endless terror. Is that what I felt when mammy died? The social worker's report states that it was me who found her, that I called the ambulance. A follow-up letter details the trauma counselling I received in the months that followed but concludes that, despite multiple methods, I refused to even acknowledge mammy's death. I can't remember much from around that time, but the pain of losing her to suicide has left me with a crippling sense of worthlessness and guilt my whole life. I can't allow another child to feel like that.

'Lyra? You hear me. Get Marie. Momma can't look after Bubba, she too weak. She not gonna last much longer.' Gloria is mumbling now, as though depleting.

'Gloria! Where are you? You've got to tell me where you are.'

'I... I don't know.' She says it quietly, resigned to her fate.

I pull myself together and stagger into the house. If Jackson knows where Gloria is he can phone 911 and send help. 'Just hang on,' I urge. 'I'm going to find Jackson, okay.'

'Please tell Miss Chloe I'm sorry,' Gloria stutters. 'Don't let Bill get away with this. Find that diary. You take it to the cops, you hear, like I oughta.'

'What does it say?' I ask, but Gloria isn't listening.

'My fault she's dead,' she slurs. 'Pushed her... over the edge. Oh Dee, oh God!' A laboured sob rips through the line, then it goes quiet.

'Gloria! You still there?'

'I was...scared. I'm sorry...so...sorry.'

'Gloria, stay awake! Keep talking to me. Tell me what the diary said.'

'Get Marie. Bubba... please... he can't...' The line goes silent again.

Realising that Jackson isn't in the lower part of the house, I thunder up the stairs. 'Jax? You up here?' The distant sound of heavy rock music, coming from his bedroom, offers a flutter of hope. I pick up the pace. 'Keep talking, Gloria,' I beg. 'Jackson will send help.'

'Tell Chloe... sorry,' mumbles Gloria. 'It...my fault.'

'It wasn't your fault.' Reaching Jackson's bedroom, I fling open the door and stop dead.

'Holy shit!'

Chapter Fifty-Four
Jackson

Jackson doesn't hear the door open. If he had, he sure as hell wouldn't be still sat on the bed with his tongue in his boyfriend's mouth. Now, with Lyra suddenly appearing in the doorway, arms hanging by her side and mouth wide open, he jumps up and smooths down his shirt. But he knows it's futile. All he wants now is for Brett to fuck off and for the room to literally just swallow him up right goddam here and now.

He tries to think of words that could fix this, but he knows there are none. His jaw clenches as he waits for her to speak first. So, it's a surprise, not to mention a relief, when he hears his... conjugation... isn't what's currently on her mind.

'It's Gloria,' says Lyra, now waving the phone at him, 'She's taken an overdose. You need to call 911.'

Jackson looks at Brett and nods for him to leave. Brett gets up, thinks about saying something, and silently obliges.

'An overdose?' Though he tries not to show it, inside Jackson is raging. *That woman has been nothing but trouble* he thinks, knowing that his dad is going to go ape shit when he finds out Gloria is still meddling into their family business. Bill had given Jackson specific orders to frighten her into silence, using violence if needed, but Jackson couldn't do it. He'd always liked Gloria; she took good care of him when she was a live-in, became almost like a surrogate mother to him. So, he'd called in a favour and had her moved to a secure location.

'Well hurry then!' yells Lyra. 'Call an ambulance.'

Jackson dials emergency services and reels off an address.

Meanwhile, Lyra is shouting down her own phone; 'Gloria! GLORIA! Shit, it's gone off!' She calls her back and slumps on the bed as the phone rings out. 'What's going on, Jackson? You've got to tell me.'

Jackson is unsure whether she means with what Lyra just saw with Brett, or with the whole Gloria situation. He chooses the more comfortable option. 'You don't need to get involved with Gloria. It's not your problem,' he says.

Lyra waves the phone at him again. 'Erm... it *is* my problem, Jax, and you need to tell me everything.'

'I can't. It's too dangerous. Just calm down.'

'Calm down? Gloria is dying while we speak, and you tell me to calm down?'

'An ambulance is on its way. I'm sure she'll be okay.'

'She'd better be.'

Jackson senses the threat in her voice.

'And you... that guy?' she continues. 'What the fuck?'

Jackson doesn't answer. He turns away and feigns interest in a letter on his desk. Inside, he's dying. *The one time you don't lock the door, you jackass.*

He hears Lyra dialling her phone again. 'Come on, Gloria,' she whispers to herself. The ringing stops and she throws the phone on the bed in frustration. 'Jackson. Talk to me. Was that the same man from The Loft that night?'

Reluctantly, Jackson turns around. 'Brett? Yeah, but listen. You'd better not tell my dad about this, okay?'

'More family secrets, eh?'

'I'm serious, Lyra. If he finds out, he'll disown me.'

'That's a bit dramatic.'

'It's true,' says Jackson, wishing for all the world that it wasn't. 'You've no idea. He would kill me! His image and reputation are everything to him.'

'More important than his son's happiness?'

'Way more!'

'I'm sorry, but your dad's an arsehole.'

'Maybe, but he's still my dad.'

There's an awkward silence before Lyra speaks again. She stares at the phone as if willing it to ring. 'Have you always been gay?' she says, finally.

'I've always known, yes.'

'Only I found something, on your laptop.'

'Found what?' he asks, shaking his head.

'Pictures of Dee, naked.'

Jackson feels the floor drop from underneath him. *Why the hell did I not delete those photos?* he thinks, cursing himself. He has no doubts that this has been the most awkward day of his entire fucking life.

'Why were you snooping on my computer?' he says, trying to deflect the question.

'Never mind that. Why for the love of God would you have nude pics of your stepmother?'

Like a finger riffling through a Rolodex, Jackson frantically searches the corners of his mind for a potentially valid reason. He exhales noisily in resignation as he realises there isn't one. He sits on the bed next to her. 'Okay, listen. To cut a long story short, Dee found out I was gay, found me in bed with the son of one of dad's business partners one night.'

'Awkward,' says Lyra, semi-jokingly.

'His dad's like mine, would have thrown him out if he'd found out. Probably would have beaten the crap out of him too. Anyway, Dee still had a bit of that hippy spirit, you know... completely open relationship, no secrets in marriage, all that crap. She said she'd *have* to tell dad. I couldn't let that happen, not just for me, for the other guy too.' He pauses, knowing the next part makes him sound like a right jackass. 'So, I blackmailed her.' As the words fill the air between them, he knows it sounds even worse spoken aloud, but what choice did he have? He remembers Dee was always nice to him, but she sure as hell wasn't going to split his family up with all that bohemian honesty bullshit.

'You blackmailed your own stepmother?' asks Lyra, incredulously.

Jackson shrugs. 'Had no choice. I'd done some digging around when dad and Dee first got together, wanted to know what kind of person I'd be sharing our house with. That's when I came across a few naked pics online from some risqué modelling she'd done when she was younger. I knew it would destroy dad if these slutty pics of his new wife did the rounds on the Cape, and so did Dee.'

'So, you kept quiet if she kept quiet, and you all lived happily ever after like one big happy family,' says Lyra with obvious sarcasm.

'Pretty much. And no, I'm not proud of it, before you ask.' Jackson feels the all-too-familiar pang of guilt. 'I think even the fact *I'd* seen the pictures caused Dee major distress, without the fear that dad might see them.'

Lyra tries calling Gloria again, but once again the phone rings out. 'I assume it was your sexuality that Chloe was referring to that day on the cliffs. When she said she was tired of covering for you and so was her mum.'

'Yeah. Chloe found out. She heard us arguing about it one night. She's been threatening to tell dad every day since. She only hasn't yet because she loves having one over on me.'

'Your sexuality doesn't define you Jax. Nor is it something to be ashamed of.'

Jackson longs to believe what Lyra is saying but can't. His father's homophobia has seen to that.

Lyra tries calling Gloria again, but she's still not picking up. 'We should go round there.'

'I told you; you're not getting involved. I've a friend who lives close. He'll go check on her.'

'And get him to let you know when the ambulance shows up,' she adds.

Jackson stands, dials a number and turns his back on Lyra. He doesn't think the day could get any worse, but if Lyra discovers the truth about *why* Gloria was paid off, he knows the shit really will hit the fan.

Chapter Fifty-Five

Lyra

'So who *exactly* was that on the phone?'

Jackson slumps down on the bed and rubs his temples, as though my questions are giving him a migraine. 'I told you. Just a guy I know who lives close.'

Being direct is obviously getting me nowhere. If Jackson wanted to protect Gloria from Bill then at least he possesses some sort of conscience, though clearly not enough to confess the truth.

'Gloria said you moved her somewhere secret because your dad wanted her hurt,' I try. 'You obviously know more than you're letting on.'

'He's my dad,' says Jackson wearily. 'It's complicated.'

I sit down beside him and scootch up until our thighs are touching. I wish I wasn't wearing this ridiculous dress now, it's just plain wrong, as bad as wearing socks with sandals.

Despite my discomfort, I try to make a connection in an attempt to open him up, choosing my words carefully and speaking softly. 'Jax, please, this is serious. Gloria might be dead right now. Do you really want that to happen?

His forehead creases as he considers the question. Just as I think he's going to spill, he veers off. 'All my life I've been trying to be the son dad wanted,' he says, still gazing away. It's a bizarre answer to the question I asked, but at least he's talking.

'You mean a clone of him?'

He nods. 'I guess. Successful, respected, popular...'

'And not gay,' I joke.

Jackson turns and winces. 'Definitely not gay. Dad's as homophobic as Ronald Reagan.'

'He's peoplephobic,' I offer, nudging him in the ribs. 'You're a million times the man he is. Kinder, nicer, way more interesting.'

'You're not flirting with me *again*, are you?'

I feel my cheeks flush until I see the smile creeping onto Jackson's face. 'I was steaming.'

'If I *was* into women, I'd have come onto you way before now.'

My throat makes a weird gurgling sound. 'I should try Gloria again.'

As expected, she doesn't answer. Jackson's revelation is a start, but how the hell am I going to get him to open up more? Going over to the window, I pick up the framed photo of Jackson with his mum and hold it up to him. 'Do you miss her?'

He shrugs. 'Didn't really know her.'

'You can still miss her though. Or at least miss the life you could have had with her.' I wander back over to the bed and sit down. I'm hoping that seeing the photo of his mum might stir something up, perhaps even encourage him to spill Bill's secret.

Jackson takes the photo and rubs his thumb over her smile. 'She looks happy, doesn't she? You can see it in her eyes.'

'She looks like the happiest woman alive.'

'So why leave?'

'I honestly can't answer that, Jax.'

'Dad says it was my fault. Says she was happy until I came along.'

I shake my head, incredulous at Bill's narcissism. 'Your dad really is an arse.'

'Tell me about it.'

'I reckon she was happy before your dad came along,' I seethe, disgusted that a so-called-parent could make his child feel responsible. 'Dee, your mom... seems your father loves to take these free-spirited women and crush them. Seems more than a coincidence that they both were desperate to leave him.'

Jackson's hands tighten around the frame, a protective gesture, I think. 'He hates mom for what she did, sees it as a betrayal to him. There are hardly any photos left of her. He cut them all up. I managed to find some and scanned them into my laptop.'

So that's who hacked Whitney's face out of the wedding photograph in Bill's desk drawer. *Sicko.*

'And your sister?'

'What about her?'

'I can see Chloe being moulded by your dad already,' I say, now more determined than ever to help Chloe with the issues she's facing.

Jackson snorts. 'I wouldn't worry. I reckon he's met his match with that one.'

Standing, Jackson wanders over to the window and carefully positions the photo back on the windowsill. He gazes at it for a moment.

I feel the words rise from the pit of my stomach. 'My mum died by suicide.' It's the first time I've ever said the words out loud.

'Jesus! Sorry I didn't know.' Jackson throws me a tight smile. 'Want to talk about it?'

I look down at my feet and realise I'm not wearing shoes. When the bejesus did that happen? 'It's not something I talk about much,' I admit, pushing down the emotions. 'I think subconsciously I've always blamed myself.

'I know what you mean,' says Jackson sullenly.

The silence that follows suggests he's withdrawing from me again.

'I'll try Marie,' I say, keen to change the subject. 'Gloria said Marie's phone was switched off but it's worth a try.'

'I'll make it right with Marie,' says Jackson, now gazing out of the window. 'I have money that dad doesn't know about. I'll make sure she doesn't struggle.'

'You shouldn't need to be paying people off for him though, Jackson! What is this all about? What does Gloria know?'

Jackson blanks the question again. He beckons me to the window. 'The minions are on the move.'

I watch a crowd of people making their way to the house. Bill is out front like the Pied Piper.

'What's happening?'

'The auction. Dad hosts it here in the house. He likes to stand on the stairs, above everyone, obviously.' Jackson glances back and rolls his eyes. 'They all bid a round of golf or a weekend in a beach home. They're all just trying to outdo each other to see who gets to suck his dick.'

I burst out laughing.

'Maybe that's what's in that mystery envelope he auctions at the end. All in the name of charity though.'

'Oh God.' I mimic sticking two fingers down my throat.

'Best go out there. You coming?'

I realise Jackson's unlikely to ever tell me the truth about Gloria, which moves me onto Plan B. 'Just going to use the bathroom first. Keep your phone on you though,' I add. 'Let me know the second you hear anything.'

Chapter Fifty-Six
Chloe

Chloe drifts across the lawn, captivated by the night. The moon hides on the horizon, a ghostly vessel resting on the high tide. Weaving her way around the side of the house, she grows stronger against the cold. The wind stings her cheeks like the back of Bill's hand, but she doesn't falter.

Chloe's breath sticks in her throat at the sound of snapping branches. She knows she must be vigilant. The enemy lurks everywhere; a thousand voices tittering in the dark.

She reaches the fire escape and counts her steps as she climbs. 'One two, Chloe's coming for you.'

She fights against the pain of the corset which digs into her ribs as she climbs higher; 'Three four, fuck you, you Irish whore.' She pushes open Bill's bedroom window and pads across the room still counting; 'Five six, you evil bitch.' Bloodied fingers trail red smears across the pristine, white walls as she pulls on the bedroom door handle and steps out onto the landing. 'Seven eight, await your fate.'

She looks down the corridor at Bill who has his back to her, the charity auction in full swing.

'Nine ten...'

Chapter Fifty-Seven
Bill

'Firstly, it's great to see so many familiar faces.' From his vantage point halfway up the stairs, Bill soaks in the sea of smiles from those packing the lounge and the spill over gathered outside that peer from the garden through open patio doors. He nods and mouths feigned gratitude at those he deems the most useful.

After a quick glance down at his notes, he clears his throat. 'As chairman of The Warren Foundation, I'd like to welcome everybody to my home... I hope you're having a lovely evening... I know I am.' He raises a glass of champagne and takes a sip. It affords him a moment of respite from holding his false smile.

'I'd also like to thank those who have supported the foundation over the years. As you know we've been instrumental in helping fund the truly great work accomplished by groups like the Martha's Vineyard Fishermen's Archive, the MV Marine Life Conversation Society, and the Chappaquiddick Arts Centre.' A smattering of polite applause breaks out.

'I'd also like to personally thank the Friends of Chappaquiddick. Without George and his stunning wife over there, Chappy wouldn't be the beautiful place it is today.'

He encourages everyone to clap in George's direction. George, a rotund man with a cheery smile, raises his hand in acknowledgement then places it over his heart and mouths 'thank-you'. *Sanctimonious prick* thinks Bill. His revulsion is tempered by the satisfaction of knowing he is the one who has the full control and attention of the crowd, everyone eager to please.

He takes another sip, but the expensive champagne is inconsequential. He feels drunk on the power. He knows there's no other feeling like it. *Better than the sex he's had with some of the women here, that's for sure*, he thinks. He spots Lydia smiling up at him adoringly. *Especially you, my dear; always first to the front when I'm talking, always first on the phone when Ted's away.*

'So, onto the auction. For those of you who don't know how it works, we have an incredible array of prizes generously gifted by local businesses. Your job is simple. Bid as much as you can to show your appreciation for all they do for The Vineyard... *your* island. Don't hold back. I know you're all wealthy and successful men.'

'And women,' a lady calls out from the back.

'And women, yes, of course. We mustn't forget our lovely wives... and girlfriends... and lovers.' He smiles, but inside he's raging as he makes a mental note of the man whose wife shouted. *There's always one fucking feminist spoiling the pack these days!*

'Okay, let the spending begin.' He consults his notes again. 'First on offer, a romantic, VIP four-course dinner for two at l'etoile. Who'll start the bidding at three hundred dollars? Twenty or so black-sleeved arms shoot up immediately.

'Three-fifty, George?

George mimics his arm being twisted behind his back, then laughs and nods as others shout to outbid him. Bill can tell this is going to go extremely well already. As usual, they're all desperate to impress, eager to appear wealthier than the next.

More importantly though, he knows none of them want to be seen as stingy in his eyes. Staying on the right side of him is why they come. They know it, he knows it. In his mind they're like Pavlov's dogs, automatically responding to any grains of significance and recognition he might care to throw their way. *It's pathetic really*, he thinks as he reflects for a moment, watching them conduct their own bidding. *Actually, it's not pathetic*, he decides. The arrangement serves both sides well. What's pathetic is them, with their humdrum lives and their neediness for approval. He'd swear that half of the men know their wives are unfaithful to their husbands with him, but they turn the other way because they know it might help further their ambition. Some of them probably even encourage it; nothing more than high-class pimps. It's a shame they're not quite as generous with their daughters. If they really wanted to score points, that's where they could really make an impression. That would certainly be a damn sight more exciting than sharing a bed with some of these hags.

'Who'll give me seven hundred? Black sleeves salute again. 'Thank-you, Fred. I knew I could rely on you. Fred beams. *If he had a tail it would be wagging by now.*

'Seven hundred and fifty?' This time arms vie for his attention again, but then immediately drop one by one. 'Come on, now. Seven fifty? Don't be shy.' *Surely they can't be giving up so soon?* he questions. *What's wrong with these cheapskates?* But there's something different. Every face in the room is staring at him, but the smiles have disappeared. Hands cover mouths. Single gasps punctuate the silence then unite in a rising wail. Eyes widen in horror. *What have I done?* thinks Bill. A finger points... but he realises it's not pointing at him, it's pointing beyond, to something behind. As he turns, Bill's heart hits the floor as he finally sees what they see.

Chapter Fifty-Eight

Lyra

Having pretended to use the bathroom, I try Chloe's bedroom door and find it unlocked. If I'm going to find the diary the time needs to be now. Thankfully the light has been left on and I carefully tread the floorboards feeling for a loose one. It's surprisingly easy to locate though harder to prise up. After two broken nails and what seems like forever, I finally unearth a dusty A5 notebook.

A tapping at the window makes me jump, but I see it's just a broken branch, its leaves clawing at the glass in the buffeting wind. Taking a deep breath, I wedge the floorboard back in place and listen at the door to make sure nobody's coming, then sit back against a wall to start reading.

My heart sinks as I read Chloe's most recent diary entry. *Oh, Chloe.* Her erratic behaviour now makes complete sense. Why didn't she just tell me? Though judging by what she's written, it's understandable she felt unable to share her secret with anybody, not to mention her own mother.

Even though the door is closed, I can hear Bill addressing the crowd; his smug, conceited voice like nails down a chalkboard. I stuff the diary into the clutch bag. This is all the evidence I need.

A sudden uproar is followed by the sound of Chloe laughing hysterically. Rushing out onto the landing, I watch in horror as she's manhandled to the ground by Bill and Jackson. Bill's harem swarm forward for front-row seats. I can't comprehend what I'm seeing; her hair has been hacked short, her face painted white, and mascara runs in identical black streaks down her face. Gone is the elegant red dress, and in its place are *my* clothes – my claret coloured basque, black leather miniskirt and fishnet tights, which have been slashed to shreds. *Is she trying to impersonate me?*

Chloe twists her head around and sees me coming down the stairs. Blood spills from her mouth as she writhes around on the stairs, thrashing out at Bill and Jackson like she's possessed.

'Lyra, stop them!' she screams.

A tiny ball of silver glints amidst the blood in her mouth and turns my stomach. She's pierced her own tongue.

'Lyra!' shouts Jackson, glancing back at me. 'Grab her.'

I can see by the redness of his eyes that he's close to tears.

Chloe manages to connect her knee with Bill's groin, causing him to let go. She then breaks free from Jackson and hauls herself to her feet. One of the guests tries to grab her as she races through the sea of horrified faces.

'Fuck you,' she spits, splattering the man's shirt and face in blood. She pushes him away, sending him crashing to the floor and drawing more screams from the now-parting crowd.

'Call Doctor Kennedy,' rasps Bill, breathless. 'He'll sedate her.'

I lean into him. 'I'm going after her,' I say through clenched teeth. 'She needs help after what she's been through, not sedating.' I glare at Bill, the implication clear.

I stride through the stunned throng who seem torn between helping their messiah or hopping in their expensive motors and getting the hell out of there. Either way, I know Chappy's elite will dine out on this night for years to come.

I shield my eyes from the driving rain as I run barefoot over the sodden grass. In the distance I can just about make out a shadowy figure sprinting towards the beach. 'Chloe, stop!'

I sprint after her until the breath in my lungs feels like glass shards, and stones bite into the soles of my feet, churned up by the angry ocean.

'Chloe. Stop!' She either doesn't hear or is choosing to ignore me. 'Chloe. Stop. I know what happened.'

She drops to the floor some twenty metres ahead, either tripping or purposely giving up the fight.

I pick my way across the sand and rocks for the last few metres and grab hold of her. Her skin is icy-cold and she's shaking all over. 'It's okay, we'll make this okay,' I say, pulling her into an embrace. 'I know what Bill did to you. Did your mum find out, Chloe? Is that why he killed her?'

Chapter Fifty-Nine
Marie

Marie glances up through the windscreen. The sky has turned an ominous black as she turns onto the sandbar carrying Seaview Avenue. As soon as she's on the sinew of land connecting OB with Edgartown, she regrets her decision.

The waters of Cow Bay have turned charcoal-grey, the wind whipping white-tipped waves that curl and froth like a boiling cauldron. She curses herself for not choosing County Road in weather like this, but she knows her mind was on other things – getting to Lyra. Since she left the Warren's, Marie has noticed a darkness whenever she thinks of her, like there are bad spirits closing in.

By the time she reaches Jaws Bridge, curtains of sea spray cascade onto the windscreen of the VW Beetle rendering the windscreen wipers useless. It reminds her of late summer, 1991, when Hurricane Bob was approaching, and driving was becoming impossible. She was younger then, of course, and braver, but she remembers the ocean swallowed so much Vineyard coastline that year the shape of the island was changed permanently. *At least it's not as bad as Bob*, she repeats to herself, trying to ease her worry.

She leans further forward in her seat, her nose nearly touching the windscreen as she tries to see the road. Suddenly, she loses control. The car begins to aquaplane over the wet surface. She grips the steering wheel tighter and braces herself for the impact as the car heads straight at the timber guard rail. But at the very last moment Marie manages to regain control. Taking a deep breath, she silently curses Bill. She's been telling him for six months now to get the tyres changed on this heap of junk. And then she's jolted as she realises she no longer works there. She also knows she shouldn't have taken the car the day she left, but she figures Bill owes her, big time.

As Sandview Avenue becomes Beach Road and Marie turns inland, she senses the barrage of trees on either side of the road closing in. *It's an omen*, she thinks, and, despite the rain beginning to fall, she presses her foot further on the accelerator knowing that she now needs to get to Lyra, fast.

Chapter Sixty
Lyra

CHLOE PULLS AWAY AND GLARES AT ME, HER EYES measuring. 'You don't know what you're talking about.'

By the way she's lisping, I suspect her tongue's swollen.

'We really need to get you to the emergency room. That'll go sceptic.'

She spits a mouthful of blood. 'I'm fine.'

Chloe averts her eyes and kicks up the sand, all the while, muddled emotions are playing out on her face.

I take the diary out of the clutch bag. 'I found this.'

She grabs it out of my hand. 'Where?'

'You know where.'

'Was it Gloria who told you about the diary?' Asks Chloe. 'I know you visited her. I heard you and Marie talking about it.'

I nod. 'Did you tell Bill that we'd visited her?'

'Yes. I had to.'

So that's why Bill framed Marie and sent Jackson round to threaten Gloria.

'Why did you visit her?'

'Because she left so suddenly. Marie was concerned.'

'I didn't even realise she was alive,' says Chloe. 'Bill told me she'd died.'

'When?'

She ponders this. 'A few weeks after mom died. He said she'd slit her wrists. Said it was my fault.'

Anger swells inside of me. 'Well he lied, Chloe. Gloria wanted me to tell you that she's sorry.' I reach out and hold both of her hands in mine. 'What was she sorry for?'

Chloe swallows. 'She wanted to go to the cops when mom... died. She knew she ought to have but Bill stopped her.'

'Because of this?' I gently take the diary from her and open it at the first page. I begin reading aloud. 'So I have a secret, one I can't share with anyone but I have to get the words down or I'll burst. Last night mom was out all evening at a lady's charity ball and Bill suggested we opened a bottle of red on the front porch. It was the most perfect evening, made more so by the wonderful company.' I stop reading and look at Chloe, wanting to gauge her reaction.

She laughs. 'The writing is crap, yeah? You can tell I didn't read as much back then. Thank God Bill came along when he did.'

Unbelievable. 'The entry is from 2019 so you were, what, thirteen?' I'm struggling to keep cool, but I know I need to if I'm going to make Chloe realise the seriousness of what comes next.

Chloe shrugs. 'Age is just a number. That's what Bill says.'

The sight of her, so small and vulnerable, with half her hair hacked off and wearing my clothes, stirs up emotions I didn't even realise I possessed. I hate Bill Warren with a passion, for many reasons, but most of all for what he's done to Chloe. I need to protect her from him if it's the last thing I do.

'You know what he did to you was illegal, right? You need to report him.'

Chloe looks at me as though I've just suggested she streak down the beach. 'No, it's not like that. Bill loves me... and I love him. Can you not see that?'

I fight the urge to slap her, reminding myself that she's only fifteen, and was thirteen when Bill began abusing her. None of this is her fault. 'Chloe, he's a grown man of fifty-six. You're a child. Surely you can see that?' I flick through a number of pages until I reach one bordered in spindly love hearts. My stomach tightens as I read. 'We made love last night. Down on the beach. It hurt a little at first but Bill says that's perfectly normal for a virgin. He whispered that he loved me over and over as he...' I throw the diary onto the sand, unable to read for a second longer. 'This is not love, it's abuse!'

Tears begin to swell in Chloe's eyes, and when her bottom lip trembles, I wrap her in my arms and hold her to me, protecting her from the rain that's now started to fall heavily. Her whole body is shaking. 'This isn't your fault, Chlo.'

'It is.' Her heart pounds against mine. She grips tighter, as though I'm her life raft and she can never let go. 'Lyra, mom died because of me.'

I kiss the top of her head and rock her in my arms. 'What happened Chloe, tell me. It's time to stop protecting Bill.'

Chapter Sixty-One
Jackson

Having just heard his dad telling everyone it's best if they go home now, Jackson feels his dad's hand on his arm, pulling him away from the crowd like he's a naughty toddler. At the same time, his phone buzzes. He yanks his arm away and holds a finger up. 'One minute,' he mouths, then turns his back on his dad, a hand over his ear to drown out the commotion of guests leaving.

It's the friend who was checking on Gloria. He tells Jackson that she's conscious and has been taken to hospital, says the cops have taken the boy to the Child Protective Services and he'll probably go into foster care for a few days.

'That sucks,' says Jackson. He feels his stomach being punched by that omnipresent ghost of separation again.

'Thanks. One more thing...,' continues Jackson. 'Go visit Gloria tomorrow and tell her everything's going to be okay. Tell her it's safe to come home now.'

Jackson hang ups and turns to face his dad whose face matches the distant thunder.

'Who was that?' asks Bill, anger reddening his face. Jackson can't recollect a time he's seen him so agitated.

'A friend.'

Bill isn't interested. *He never is*, thinks Jackson. His dad grips his arm again. Jackson reasons that it probably helps him feel he's still in control. 'Find Lyra and Chloe,' his dad hisses. 'Bring them both to the tool room in the garage.'

Jackson doesn't respond. He stares into his dad's eyes and sees they're dark, cold and lifeless. There's no warmth, no compassion, no concern for Jackson in all of this. In that moment he realises that he's no more than just a tool, a handy pocketknife his dad carries round for multiple purposes. But not one of its functions has anything to do with being a son. Jackson knows his dad sees him as a gofer, driver, messenger, fixer, assailant and cleaner-upper.

Right now, with that clarity of thought, it feels like an epiphany, and that there's no reason to pretend anymore. He's merely the person called on to fetch, carry and conceal. While Jackson does the heavy lifting his dad gets the respect. Jackson is the one whose hands get dirty so his dad's stay clean.

The immediate lifting of loyalty feels like a huge weight has lifted from Jackson's shoulders.

'No.' he says to his dad with a force that even surprises himself.

Bill leans in, eyes narrowed. 'What did you say?'

'I said no. I'm not doing this anymore.'

'You'll do as I say.' Bill says it slowly, a threat implied.

Jackson removes his dad's hand from his arm.

'It's over, dad,' he says, shaking his head. 'I'm done.'

Bill stares, sneering for a moment then points his finger in Jackson's face. 'We're through,' he says, then turns and heads out through a side door, away from the departing guests. Jackson feels no emotion, no fear of retribution, no sense of loss.

He might be through, thinks Jackson, *but I'm not*. There's still one more thing he needs to do, something he now knows he should have done in the beginning. He stabs at his phone. The response is quick.

'I want to report a murder,' he answers.

Chapter Sixty-Two

Bill

Bill slams the door behind him. He knows it's more than just out of anger, it's a deliberate, figurative act. *Fides supra omnes* - loyalty above everything. *Without it, you're a waste of my time, just like that stupid punk girl from Ireland*, he thinks.

He rues the day he invited Lyra to stay, regrets allowing Chloe to talk him into it. He thinks about how life would have been so much simpler if she hadn't have come. Chloe would have continued to bury her hormonal outbursts and he wouldn't have suffered the indignity of being embarrassed in front of the whole island.

There's no doubt in his mind that Chloe has gone too far this time. *Enough is enough*, he thinks. He's decided Doctor Kennedy will give her something from his little bag of tricks to stop all this nonsense. Why wouldn't he? Like most of The Vineyard, he has no choice. Besides, the doctor owes him a favour or two.

A flash of lightning splits the sky as Bill crosses the garden lawn and heads straight to the beach. There's a place where he knows Chloe usually sits when she's in one of her teenage moods, and he's sure that's where he'll find the two of them now.

He listens for voices but all he can hear is a barrage of white noise from the rustling of trees either side. A fierce gust of wind tries to push Bill back, but he battles on as leaves, chair cushions and linen napkins spin around him in a frenzied dance.

With every stride into the headwind his anger grows. He distinctly remembers telling Lyra not to talk about Dee when he left her to unpack the day she arrived, but like all young people, she thought she knew better. He hopes she's damn-well proud of herself now with all the mess she's created.

Bill thinks about all the things he's done for Lyra - taken her places, offered her his home, his food, paid for nice dresses, tried to improve her. At this moment in time, he can't recollect having met anyone that's quite as ungrateful, and there's no way he's letting such an insignificant little brat ruin everything he's worked for all his life. As he nears the end of the garden and hears the rush of surf, he knows one thing's for sure... after he finds Lyra tonight, she won't be saying another word about this to anyone ever again.

Chapter Sixty-Three
Lyra

Chloe slumps down onto the wet sand and rakes her fingers through her bedraggled hair. The surf tumbles over and over some ten metres away. Blankets of hissing froth stretch to reach us before being yanked back by the angry ocean. 'He did a bad thing.' She gazes up at me, her eyes wide but wary. She wants to trust me, I know it.

Crouching beside her, I grab her hand and hold it in both of mine. 'Go on.'

'He loves me, Lyra. I swear he does.' Another gleam of tears well in her eyes.

'It's okay, Chloe. I know,' I lie, desperate for her to spit out the truth. Did your mum find out?'

Chloe nods.

'Fuck!'

'Gloria found my diary.'

'And she gave it to your mum?'

Chloe averts her gaze. She doesn't need to confirm.

'Jeez, Chlo! Why didn't you tell the cops?'

Before Chloe can answer, a distant shout raises the hairs on the back of my neck. Chloe hears it too. Without warning, she scrambles to her feet and runs along the beach into the darkness.

'Chloe!' I chase after her, my limbs working hard against the wind and wet sand. The beach narrows until it's just a few metres wide. The ocean rushes over my feet and spills into the lagoon, before it's clawed back, trying to drag me with it. Then there is no more beach, the thin spit of land that connects Chappy to the mainland severed by the storm. I look around. The ocean has surrounded me, pushing and pulling my legs in all directions. Behind me, a figure bounds out of the dark.

'Get in the water. It's Bill. He'll kill us. Chloe is already submerged up to her waist. The current is dragging her out, the storm kicking up two-metre waves. I know if I follow her in, I'll either freeze or drown. If I stay, Bill will be on me in seconds.

I wade deeper into the water, barely feeling the icy coldness. The current immediately picks me up and pushes me towards Chloe. I reach out and grip hold of her. We're both dragged further out and can no longer stand up, the waves incessant as they rise and break every second. 'I don't swim well, Chlo,' I splutter. The ocean rips us apart and washes over my head. My breath comes in heavy gasps, my body numb with shock.

Chloe manages to swim closer and grabs my hand, pulling us together again. She slips her hand under my arms to keep me up, our faces inches apart. Our legs entangle as I try to kick back towards the shore.

'It'll be easier if you let go,' I say, struggling to keep above the surface. But instead of loosening her grip, I feel Chloe's arm tightening around my chest.

'Let go,' I scream, desperate to keep my chin above the water.

'You want to take Bill from me, don't you?' she cries above the ocean roar. 'Just like mom did.'

Before I realise what she's doing, her hand is on my head and I'm enveloped in silence below the surface, anchored by her weight. I try to wrestle free, my lungs empty of air, but it's futile. At that moment I accept that I will drown. I try to scream but only an explosion of air bubbles emerge as the salty water fills my mouth.

Chapter Sixty-Four
Chloe

She can thrash all she wants, Chloe thinks, knowing from experience that soon Lyra's body will go limp and it will all be over.

Bill is screaming Chloe's name, his legs submerged up to his knees. Chloe doubts he'll risk coming any further. Swimming has never been his forte.

Though he's a damn sight better than mommy dearest ever was.

'Let her go, Chloe! Let her go, now!'

Silly Bill. Why can't he see that Lyra's death will be a blessing? She'd have only manipulated him and spent all of his money like every woman before her. Poor Bill, he's a magnet for gold diggers.

Somehow, likely due to a brief slip in Chloe's concentration, Lyra manages to break free. Chloe watches with amusement as the Irish whore coughs and splutters as she attempts to reach the shore. For somebody who grew up around water, she sure as hell can't swim. Chloe counts to three in her head.

One Mississippi, two Mississippi...

And then glides effortless to where Lyra is thrashing around like an injured seal. Yanking her back by the hair, Chloe shoves Lyra's head under the water. 'Die bitch!'

It's sad really, Chloe muses. She really liked Lyra in the beginning, even believed that the two of them could be friends. It would have been nice to have a friend, they could have enjoyed peanut butter and jelly sandwiches, wrote poetry, and plaited one another's hair. Chloe's mom was the best at braids. In fact, it's the thing she misses most about her mother.

The bundle of bones in Chloe's grasp begins to weaken. About time.

It was three months after Dee told Chloe that she was leaving Bill that Chloe finally killed her.

Initially she was reluctant, despite being desperate to stay with Bill and have him all for herself. Dee was, after all, pretty useful to have around. Not only was she good at braids, but she also made a mean hot chocolate. But after much deliberation, Chloe concluded that Gloria's hot beverages were passable, and she could teach her to braid with just a little patience.

She sees Bill wading in the water fully-clothed. His tuxedo will be ruined and he only had it tailored last week. Thankfully, Lyra has stopped her carry-on and a succession of air bubbles are rising to the surface.

'Let her go. Chloe! The cops. They're on their way.' The cold is stealing the words straight out of Bill's mouth. The poor man is going to catch his death.

'As you like.' Chloe lets the home wrecker sink to the ocean bed but keeps alert in case she suddenly bobs back up to the surface. She certainly wouldn't put it past the chancer. Chloe smiles at her clever choice of word. Lyra had great colloquialisms.

Bill is now gaining ground and spluttering her name between mouthfuls of water. Chloe worries that the current is too strong for him. 'Go back,' she shouts, concerned that he might drown. How ironic would that be?

She wishes more than anything that the stories in her diary were true; when she closes her eyes she can almost feel Bill's strong arms around her, his lips pressed hard onto hers. Chloe's plan *had* been to drown her mother in the ocean, it would have been a cleaner kill and made the suicide cover-up more believable. The date had been set and the groundwork was underway, but then that daft bitch Gloria had found the diary and kicked up a fuss by showing it to Dee. When Dee had tearfully asked Chloe if the contents were true, and Chloe had said yes, Dee went all cuckoo on her.

'That bastard! We're leaving right now,' her mother had screeched, clearly high as a kite from too much gin and depression meds. That had been Chloe's doing too. It was easy to convince her mother she was suffering from depression; the odd orchestrated argument between her mother and Bill, gluing her mom's HRT patches over the top of nicotine patches (that sent her positively batshit) - oh and her greatest move ever - adding bulking powder to Dee's morning smoothie. The more weight she gained, the more repulsed Bill was, and well, her mother likely *was* depressed when she finally took her fat ass to the doctor!

'Lyra! Holy shit. Chloe, help me get her out!'

Bill has somehow managed to drag Lyra's corpse up off the seabed and is swimming to shore with her underneath his arm. She looks kinda cool actually, like a life-size rag doll.

Her work now done, Chloe glides past Bill and his Corpse Bride, (hell, she's funny).

Retrieving the diary buried in the sand, Chloe heads in the direction of the house. Though she's pretty sure Bill was bluffing when he threatened her with the cops, she decides to make contingency plans just in case.

Chapter Sixty-Five
Bill

Bill drags Lyra's lifeless body onto the wet sand and slaps her hard across the face. 'Wake up! WAKE. UP!' He feels his pulse pounding as the panic rises. One death on his property is bad enough, but two - and both by drowning! That's a headache he doesn't need.

January 7th had been a strange sort of day. Dee had been less than impressed with Bill's anniversary gift - a 2.5 carat diamond necklace no less. She'd gifted him a bottle of Henry Jacques cologne which, as far as Bill was concerned, was a metaphorical slap in the face. No thought had gone into the gift whatsoever.

Bill tips Lyra's head back and brings his mouth down onto hers. He performed the exact same task on his late wife when he'd dragged her lifeless body out of his swimming pool a little over six months ago. He places one hand on top of the other and presses down on Lyra's chest. 'Breathe, damn it. Breathe.'

Once again, déjà vu causes Bill to shudder. It was while he was chanting the same words to Dee that Chloe had dropped her bombshell.

'You're wasting your time,' she said, matter-of-factly, herself fully-dressed and sopping wet. 'She was at the bottom for at least five minutes. Even if you manage to bring her back, she'll be a cabbage. I'm sure you wouldn't want that.'

Bill looked up at his stepdaughter, aghast. 'Did you do this?'

Chloe smiled, but it was the vacuous depth in her eyes that made Bill shudder.

'Jesus. Why?'

'She was planning to leave you.' Chloe's head cocked to the side as though genuinely confused by Bill's reaction. 'She was going to take me away from you... I love you, Bill. You love me. We're soulmates. 'Nobody' is going to keep us apart.'

Leaving his wife's lifeless body poolside, Bill sprinted towards the house.

'What are you doing?' Catching up with him, Chloe gripped Bill's wrist and yanked him round. 'Mom killed herself. She was depressed. I even have a suicide note. Well, a poem. It was the best I could do.' She was excited, waiting for Bill to realise how smart she'd been. 'Come on, Bill. This is a good thing.'

Bill prised her hands off him. 'You're not right, Chloe. I'm calling the police. You've killed your own mother, for God's sake!'

Once in the house, Bill dialled a nine and a one and then stopped dead. 'What did you say?'

'I said I sure hope Gloria doesn't tell them about my diary,' repeated Chloe.

'Come on, punk. Don't do this to me.'

Pressing his fingers underneath Lyra's chin, Bill thinks he feels a pulse. He pumps her chest over and over, before placing his mouth onto her cracked, rough lips and blowing hard. Still, she doesn't breathe.

In contrast Bill's breathing quickens. He has to admit there's something quite arousing about giving the punk mouth-to-mouth. He tries again, this time savouring the salty taste on her blue lips. One last go, he thinks, and if there's still no response, he'll be left with no choice other than to dump her out at sea and feign ignorance to her whereabouts. It's risky but he figures he'd get away with it.

After all, it wouldn't be the first time.

Chapter Sixty-Six
Lyra

I sit up, choking and spluttering.

'You're okay. Get it all up.'

I'm vaguely aware the voice is Bill's, and that he's wrapped his suit jacket around me and is rubbing circles on my back. My throat and nose burn with saltwater and each breath causes excruciating pain in my lungs. I feel myself losing consciousness.

A sharp sting across my cheek rouses me. 'You have to try and stand. We need to get help.'

I nod, though when I attempt it, my muscles seize causing me to stumble into Bill.

'Come on,' he urges, now holding me up. 'Try and walk.'

The dress I'm wearing is as heavy as lead and no matter how hard I try I can't move forward, as though I'm trying to run in a dream.

'Stay with me Lyra,' says Bill, wheezing. 'Chloe's gone; we have to find her.'

A sudden awareness shakes me to the core. *Chloe practically admitted to killing her mother and then tried to drown me.*

I fall to my knees and feel as though I'm plummeting through a black hole.

'Get up!' I open my eyes and see Bill's face inches from mine. 'Stay. Awake.' His words are forceful, but welcome. It means I'm not dead. He hauls me back onto my feet and slides his arms through mine. 'You have to try and walk,' he says. 'To keep awake.'

'It was Chloe, wasn't it?' I rasp, every word grating the back of my throat. 'She killed her mother and made it look like suicide, didn't she?'

Bill doesn't reply though I can see his brain working overtime.

'I found her diary.'

'Where?' Bill's eyes flash with anticipation. 'Give it to me!'

I scan the beach. 'I think she took it.'

Bill lets go of me and runs towards the shore. I stand shivering for what feels like hours. Eventually he returns empty handed. 'Damn. It isn't there. She must have taken it. It was all make-believe,' he adds as an afterthought. 'She made it all up.'

'If it was all just a fantasy, why go to such lengths to silence Gloria?'

'Because she believed it!' Bill's voice rises in exasperation. 'I couldn't risk her going to the police.'

I allow Bill to pull me the length of the beach, the two of us having now fallen into a stunned silence. It's only as we reach the Warren's lawn that I speak again.

'I believe you about the diary. What I don't understand is how you could have allowed her to get away with murder?' I'm genuinely surprised that a man of Bill's power and influence could be blackmailed by a teenage girl. 'Not to mention allowing her to remain living here. What were you thinking?'

Chapter Sixty-Seven
Bill

'What was I thinking?' says Bill. 'I was thinking I didn't want to go to jail for a crime I didn't commit.'

Movement to the left of the beach house triggers the security lights. The punk practically jumps into Bill's arms. 'Shit,' she squarks. 'It's her.'

Bill prises her hand off his arm. 'Not necessarily. But if it is,' he adds after a moment, 'that means she not in the main house. We'll use the phone in there.'

The punk isn't for moving. 'She wants to fecking kill me!'

'You're safe, you're with me now,' says Bill in the hope of placating her. He seriously does not need her freaking out right now.

'So let me get this straight,' says the punk, now stumbling beside Bill at a snail's pace. 'Why did Dee write a suicide note if she didn't commit suicide?'

'That was Chloe's doing,' says Bill with just a hint of pride. He doesn't condone what Chloe did, not by any stretch, but he has to give the girl credit for craftiness. If only his own child possessed such ingenuity. 'It was a poem. Chloe and her mother loved poetry and would often set each other little challenges. Chloe chose the title, *tired of life*, for her mother and stored it away. Genius really.'

'That's just sick,' says the punk. 'So it was all premeditated? That makes it even worse.'

Bill *had* thought it preferable to play the accidental death story to the cops. It seemed rather unbelievable to him that somebody terrified of water would choose to bind their ankles together with a tie and throw themselves into a swimming pool. Surely there were nicer ways to kill yourself? But in the end, Chloe had convinced him that suicide would be investigated with much less vigour than an alleged accident, especially given Dee's history of depression and a suicide note in Dee's handwriting. Bill therefore helped his stepdaughter to tie her dead mother's ankles together with his own silk tie, and the two of them threw her back into the pool. They waited until the morning before alerting the cops. As already stated, Bill wasn't overly comfortable with the plan, but he couldn't risk the cops believing Chloe's tales, especially if she was backed up by Gloria. And besides, Dee was dead. Nothing was going to bring her back, and in truth, it was somewhat of a blessing to Bill. Dee had become incredibly ungrateful, and he'd suspected she was close to asking for a divorce even before Chloe had confirmed it. Of course, he never would have allowed Dee to leave. His late wife Whitney had already tried to pull that stunt some years before, threatening to take his son and heir with her. He'd become very upset by Whitney's rudeness, which led to him stabbing her repeatedly in the heart and dumping her body at sea. He was aware that it would have looked suspicious if two of his wives vanished without a trace, so yes, in a roundabout way, his stepdaughter had done him a favour.

Chapter Sixty-Eight

Lyra

Bill opens the door to the main house, seemingly oblivious to my shock. How can he speak about the murder of his wife at the hands of his stepdaughter so calmly?

'Come on,' he orders when I remain frozen on the porch. 'You need to change out of that dress or you'll freeze.'

'What if Chloe's in there?'

Bill peers into the dark interior. 'I can't hear anything.'

Once inside, Bill flicks on the light. I flinch as he does, almost expecting Chloe to lunge out at me like in a horror film.

'I'll do a quick scan of the bottom floor,' says Bill, now heading for the lounge.

I remain in the foyer, dripping wet and shivering from cold and fear. I feel I should grab a knife from the kitchen for my own protection, but fear has bolted my feet to the floor.

'She's not downstairs,' relays Bill a moment later, his wet shoes squeaking on the marble floor. It reminds me that, despite him being completely away with the fairies, he did save my life. At least he isn't a cold-blooded murderer like his step-daughter, though that's the only positive I can grant him. 'I'll head up and change,' he says without an apparent care in the world. 'She might be sulking in her bedroom.'

Sulking? Is he for fecking real? 'Bill, you do realise that she tried to kill me, right?' I try and fail to keep my voice level. 'If it wasn't for you, I'd be floating at the bottom of the Atlantic.'

He smiles as though acknowledging a thanks. 'She does let her emotions run away with her at times. Teenagers for you. I won't be a minute.' He heads upstairs without a backward glance, leaving me utterly speechless.

'She's not upstairs.'

Several minutes later, I breathe relief as Bill reappears, now changed from his sopping-wet suit to a beige cashmere jumper and jeans. 'Here.' He passes me a bundle of clothes which consist of lacy underwear, a pair of pressed trousers and a silk blouse.

I stare at them, aghast.

'They were Dees from before she piled on the weight. They look like they'll fit,' he says flippantly, and retrieves his mobile from his jeans pocket. I suddenly remember mine was in the clutch bag, now lost at sea. 'Just ringing a doctor friend of mine,' he continues. 'He's supposed to be coming to give Chloe something that'll calm her down.' He turns away from me, the phone now pressed to his ear.

'And the police? Please say you're calling the police?'

Bill glances back at me and shakes his head. 'Have you not been listening to anything I've just said? People can't know about this. I'm a very private man.'

'People *do* know about it, Bill. They saw what happened at the party.'

'And that's *all* they saw. A silly teenage tantrum.'

I can't speak, as though I'm drowning all over again. 'You can't just let her get away with it!' I manage to spit out. 'She's crazy. A psychopath.'

Bill angrily stabs at the phone. 'Damn voicemail. Look, Lyra,' he says, speaking slowly as though I'm mentally incapacitated. 'I know you had this fanciful idea that you were going to come here and save Chloe and write a million-dollar bestseller, but you haven't done either, in fact you've made a bad situation worse, so I think the best thing all round, for everybody, is that you just pack your things and leave.'

This is absurd. How the hell does he expect me to leave with the knowledge I now possess? 'Bill, you've just admitted that your stepdaughter killed your wife! We have to tell the police.'

'Absolutely not,' he barks. 'Don't forget I covered it up.'

'I'll be able to vouch for you,' I try. 'They will understand why you did it.'

Bill squeezes shut his eyes and when he opens them again, I see a flash of irritation. 'Do you want Chloe to go to jail for the rest of her life? They'll try her as an adult you know. Do you really want her to rot in prison?'

'Yes!' I can't stop my voice from rising. I take a deep breath and continue more calmly, knowing that I can't lose my head right now. 'Bill, we *have* to call the police. She's dangerous. She probably won't even go to jail. She has serious mental health problems.' I'm doubtful of this, believing it's much more likely that Chloe is a born psychopath, but that isn't for me to decide.

'It's called Erotomania,' says Bill with a hint of pride, before continuing to scroll through a list of contacts on his phone. 'I've researched it. She believes I'm in love with her, sees what she wants to see. I've been trying to redirect her thinking, help her to realise that I love her but not in the way she thinks. Ah, here we go.' He holds the phone to his ear. 'This doctor owes me a favour too.'

'She orchestrated her own mother's death for Christ's sake!'

Bill holds up a finger, silencing me. It dawns on me that he likely enjoys Chloe's obsession with him. It'd certainly feed his egotism.

I hear the phone ring out. 'Where are all the doctors when you need one.' Bill blows out an exasperated breath.

'You're insane. I'm calling the police.' I make a swipe for his mobile.

Bill is quick to react, moving the mobile out of my reach. 'I seriously wouldn't do that if I were you.'

I stare at him until he blinks.

'How much?'

'What?'

'How much to make you forget about all this. Name your price. A hundred thousand? Two hundred?'

I clench my fists. 'Nothing. I can't be bought.'

'You can and you will.' A mix of anger and humour flashes in Bill's eyes. He really is the smuggest bastard I've ever encountered. 'Five hundred.'

'No.'

He leans in really close. 'One. Million.'

He thinks he's got me. The triumph is there is his barely suppressed smirk. Power and control. It's what Bill Warren feeds off. I swallow hard. 'I. Cannot. Be. Bought.'

His eyes turn on a sixpence from amused to incensed. 'You can and you will!' The ferocity in his voice makes me jump. 'I've worked hard my whole life to build up my good standing here and I'll not have some jumped-up little slut ruining it for me.' He turns away and I watch his chest rising and falling. When he turns back around, something inside of him has changed, as though a flick has switched.

There is now no emotion behind his eyes.

Chapter Sixty-Nine
Chloe

Chloe watches from behind a Maple tree as Marie's tin can pulls up outside the beach house. *Meddling bitch.* If it wasn't for her, Chloe and Lyra would have been best friends by now. She was even considering asking Lyra to be maid of honour at her and Bill's wedding.

Closing her eyes, Chloe imagines marrying Bill, the back of her eyelids now a waterfront wedding. She pictures herself floating down the aisle in a flowing white wedding dress, Bill's eyes burning with love as he says, *I do.* Her thoughts turn to their wedding night, the two of them together in soul and body for the first time; Bill's fingers exploring every inch of her, just like the stories in her diary. She lays her hand flat on her breast and feels the beating of her heart. It's pounding so quickly she thinks she might explode.

Her eyes snap open. A hatred mixed with intense jealousy tightens her chest. Why did Bill risk his life to save Lyra? Has that Irish bitch really poisoned his mind so much that he'd drown for her, leaving Chloe alone?

Chloe's eyes trail Marie as she unlocks the door to the beach house. Moments later, she sees the ex-housekeeper's silhouette appear at Lyra's bedroom window. *Trespasser* thinks Chloe. Marie has no right to be in Lyra's room.

Chloe considers the probability that it was Marie who encouraged Lyra to go after Bill; it makes perfect sense. If Lyra was Bill's wife she'd insist on cooking and cleaning like her mother did, leaving Marie to sit on her fat ass reading the bible. That's what she's likely doing now; sprinkling holy water on the bedspread so Bill and Lyra can fuck with the Lord's blessing.

Chloe marches over to the beach house and enters the kitchen. The carving knife slides easily out of its holder and she grins as she holds it up to her face. 'Time to meet your beloved maker, Marie,' she whispers.

Chapter Seventy

Lyra

'No amount of money will be enough, Bill,' I say, refusing to flinch as he continues to glare at me. 'You can't buy your way out of this one.'

'Why do you even care?' The question seems to explode out of him, as though he genuinely can't comprehend it. I guess in Bill's world, people aren't big on morals, him included.

'Chloe killed her mother. She tried to kill me and she'll kill again. I can't let that happen.'

'She won't. I can handle her.'

'Like you handled her this evening when she was moments away from drowning me!' I shout, no longer able to control myself.

A vein in Bill's neck bulges. 'You either leave of your own accord... *with* a pile of money... or I'll make it happen!'

'How? Kill me? You couldn't stand the backlash.' My hands are shaking from pure rage.

Bill emits a sickening laugh. 'It wouldn't be the first time. You really think I let Jackson's mom walk away from me?'

I edge backwards, his admission blackening the space between us. Bill continues to stare at me with the same vacant intensity.

I turn and scramble out of the open door into a lash of wind and use my final shred of strength to run in the direction of the beach house.

I hear Bill behind me, breathlessly calling my name. I plough on. If I can make it to the beach house before him, I can call the police from the phone in there. And then what? Will Bill kill me before they arrive? And where the hell is Jackson, not to mention Chloe?

I look the length of the drive. Should I run onto the road and call for help? Though this is Chappy, Bill's kingdom. Who in their right mind would stop and protect me?

And then I spot Marie's car.

Shit! The door to the beach house is wide open. Instinctively I race inside and hear Marie screaming from upstairs.

I practically fall up the stairs, calling out to her, certain that Chloe must be in the house too.

I stumble into the bedroom where Chloe has her back to me, hammering on the ensuite door. Marie must have locked herself inside.

'Chloe!' Her name comes out as a strangled plea.

She turns around, unnervingly slow, and smiles, her lips fixed in a tight sneer.

I see the splintered stab marks in the door first, and then my eyes fall down to her hand.

'Oh! Hi, Lyra,' she says, running the knife along the palm of her hand. 'I really thought you'd be dead by now.'

Chapter Seventy-One
Chloe

Lyra suddenly darts from the bedroom, which leaves Chloe pondering an annoying choice. *Does she finish Marie first, or does she go and get Lyra? What would be most fun?* She weighs it up for a second, stares at the damaged bathroom door, then chases after Lyra.

As she reaches the top of the stairs, she sees Lyra at the bottom, falling over herself in an effort to get away. Lyra looks up over her shoulder, her eyes wide like a rabbit in a headlight... *or maybe like a leprechaun... fucking Irish bitch*, thinks Chloe. 'Lyra, wait for me,' she calls out as if they were friends in a schoolyard.

Chloe closes the gap by taking the stairs three at a time, but Lyra is still just out of reach. Lyra stumbles to the open front door, whimpering as she sees Chloe has caught up with her. Chloe slashes at her shoulder with the knife and Lyra instinctively bobs her head forward. The blade connects, but only the tip. A thin red line begins to widen at the bottom of her neck.

The swinging of the knife throws Chloe off balance allowing Lyra to move out of reach again. Then just as she reaches the front door, Lyra slips in a pool of rainwater blown in from the storm.

Her legs slide sideways from under her, and she falls to the floor on her back.

Chloe stands over her, one leg either side. 'That was hilarious!' she says, laughing.

Lyra holds her hands outstretched in a pathetic act of defence. 'Chloe, Chloe... it's me, Lyra...' she snivels.

'I *know* who the fuck you are,' says Chloe. Her face is serious now, the knife raised. '*You're* the bitch who tried to steal my Bill.'

'I didn't, please... I swear to God... don't...'

Chloe smiles. She likes seeing Lyra like this. *Why couldn't she have been so tame before*, she thinks, *instead of coming on like the big I am, looking down on me with her fancy author words and patronising sympathy*? 'I liked you at first, Lyra,' she says, 'but then you became just like the rest of them with your *poor Chloe* this and your *Chloe's a whack job* that. I hear what everybody says, you know. When are you all going to realise, there's nothing wrong with me? It's you lot that are crazy.'

'You're right,' says Lyra, her breaths quick and sharp. 'It's us... we all need help.' She starts to slither backwards out the front door, arms still raised. 'You need to help us.'

'Too late,' snaps Chloe. She brings the knife down with all her force towards Lyra's belly. But the blade doesn't sink in with that satisfying squashy feeling. It stops mid-air. And Chloe sees there are somebody else's hands around hers. And that they're male hands. And that Bill is here. He's stood over Lyra, his fingers gripped around Chloe's. Lyra clambers to her feet.

'Give it to me,' he says quietly, his eyes inches from Chloe's face. She stares into Bill's beautiful pools of smoky grey and can see the love. *It's there, it's always been there. He knows it, and I know it*, she thinks. *It's just stupid bitches like Lyra and my mom who refuse to accept it.* And that's why she knows for certain that Lyra has to go.

Chloe loosens her grip as though she's going to give Bill the knife, then quickly thrusts it forward into Lyra's chest with all her strength. This time Chloe feels the satisfactory sensation of steel perforating muscle and splintering bone. She watches Lyra's eyes widen with shock as she pushes it deeper and deeper. *Bye-bye bitch.*

With a half-smile, she glances at Bill, seeking his approval, his acknowledgement of her all-consuming love for him. But there is no smile, no approval. All she sees are eyes probing, questioning. *Why?* She wonders. She looks down. Instead of seeing Lyra's dress soaked in red, blood pours from Bill's jumper.

Chloe lets go of the handle and snaps her head towards Lyra, who stands frozen to the spot. Their eyes lock for a second, then Lyra stumbles backwards out the door, turns and runs.

Chapter Seventy-Two
Jackson

Jackson closes his eyes and imagines his head sinking deeper into the pillow. If the melancholia of Elizabeth My Dear, his go-to band for relaxing, doesn't take his mind off all the craziness, he knows nothing will.

That sixth sense won't fade or sway
That someday you'll just breakaway

He opens his eyes, suddenly finding new meaning in the lyrics. He'd always thought the song was about breaking up with somebody, but now realises it's a bigger theme than that. It's about a turning point in life. And for Jackson, he knows now is that time to break free, to turn off the route that somebody else has mapped for him. The thought both excites and worries him. Having been pushed and pulled by his dad for so long, he's not sure he knows how to take control, make his own decisions, and decide what's right for him and him alone. *Well, I'm about to find out*, he thinks, *that 911 call has made sure of that.*

He removes his Air Pods and wanders to the window. *How long do they take?* Then it dawns on him that the cops may not come at all, such is dad's influence on the island. But for murder? Surely they have to come.

He tries to imagine his dad's face when they put crazy Chloe in handcuffs and bundle her into a cop car. Will there be relief? Anger? Sympathy? *Knowing Dad, there'll probably be nothing*, he thinks, *just a reminder to the chief about the next fundraiser he'll be expected to attend*.

He believed his dad when he said Chloe had made all that stuff up in the diary, Jackson knows she does have some weird crush on him, it's obvious to those that know her. Despite that, he knows he should have said no when his dad wanted his help in paying off Gloria. What he didn't realise, at least not at first, was that Chloe had killed Dee. He genuinely thought she'd taken her own life after believing her husband was abusing her daughter. But of course the house has walls, and Jackson isn't stupid. It soon became obvious to him what had really happened that night, but how could he prove it? Dee had long since been cremated and Jackson knew the cops would never reopen the case. Chloe knew that Jackson had figured it out, he could tell by the sly smirks she'd throw his way whenever Dee was mentioned. *Sick bitch.* 'I guess we both have to look out for each other now, Jax,' she'd say sweetly. What she really meant was, *you know I'm a murderer and I know you're queer. I won't tell if you don't.*

Well now he *has* told. Whatever does or doesn't happen as a result is out of his hands.

Jackson actually thinks that being arrested is probably the best thing that could happen to Chloe. Yes, she's a psycho, but she seriously needs help, has done for a long time. Maybe at last she'll get it, he hopes. He knows his dad should have had her checked out way sooner but he was always afraid of what Chloe might say to a shrink, and that would take the control away from his dad.

It makes him sad when he thinks about Lyra. It's possible he might never see her again. He's sure his dad will have most likely offered her a ton of money to disappear and forget all about this and she'll just go back to her cosy life in Ireland never to mention it again. Jackson believes that under different circumstances they could have become good friends. He likes her spirit, particularly the fact that she's spunky enough to be true to herself and not give a shit what others think. *Unlike me*, he thinks. He knows it was true what he said to her tonight after she saw him with Brett – if he was into women, he and Lyra would have got something going.

Suddenly the outside lights turn on, illuminating the driving rain in hazy cones of phosphorous yellow. *The police must be here*, he thinks. But then... *what the hell?* he spots Lyra running up the drive. She has no shoes, looks terrified, constantly checking over her shoulder. He goes to open the window but then stops when he sees another figure chasing her, and there's no mistaking who that is, or that it's a knife she's carrying in her hand.

Chapter Seventy-Three
Lyra

The same thought loops my mind as I trample over sodden grass... *I don't want to die. I don't want to fucking die!*

I glance back over my shoulder and see the vague, shadowy image of Chloe in the dazzle of floodlights. She isn't running, yet somehow she's gaining ground. Or is it a trick of the mind? At least if she's chasing *me*, Marie is safe.

Through the driving rain, the main house comes into focus, yet it still seems a million miles away. I push on, my breath coming in gasps, every muscle in my arms and legs now straining in survival mode.

She was intending to kill me, again, and would have succeeded if Bill hadn't stood in the way. Though I'm certain it wasn't intentional.

It happens so quickly that it barely registers when I fall face-first into the damp earth, my mouth and nose clogged with mud. I'm sure pain follows, but all I feel is a cold numbness, disorientated in both body and mind as I roll onto my back and stare up at a snare of tree branches that whisper a forewarning; move or die.

I attempt to stand but my ankle buckles beneath me, and then the throbbing in my leg radiates through my entire body; I suck in breath through gritted teeth and crawl, dragging my body out of the glare, knowing that I need to hide in the trees. My fingers press against something hard - the aviary.

From the shadows, I catch a flash of movement and then the rustling of leaves. And then I hear Chloe's singsong voice. 'Coming Lyra, ready or not.'

Terror thrums through my veins as I manage to scramble inside. I close the door slowly, quietly. It shuts so far and then jams on a dead bird.

'Lyraaa?' The voice is closer

I move round onto my back, my eyes stinging from the pain in my leg, and back-up against the cage. Rain pummels the roof and surrounding trees in an unrelenting riot of blows. The stench of rotting flesh rising from the floor causes me to gag. Why didn't I run when she killed the birds? I bite down hard on my lip, feel the warm trickle of blood in my mouth.

Pulling my knees up to my chest, I hug myself tight. My mind overcome with pain and the events of tonight. I keep my eyes fixed on the gap in the door, tremors rocking my entire body.

The pain ceases as a memory takes over.

'Mammy, mammy.'

I tiptoe across the carpeted floor, my feet like ice pops. The room is dark save for a slice of light in the door. I peep out, panic filling me like I'm a balloon ready to pop.

Mammy is tightening a belt around her arm. She has been poorly for longer than days, maybe even weeks, because the demons are back, the ones that chain her to the bed all day and cause her to cry out all night.

She burns something on a spoon. I hold in my breath, not making a sound. I mustn't cry. I mustn't make a sound. She fills a needle and smacks her wrist.

Quietly I turn around and tiptoe back to bed.

Breath rushes out of my lungs as the aviary door creaks open, snapping me from the trance.

'Found you.'

Chloe stands over me, panting through gritted teeth. Her eyes are as wild as the twisted strands of wet hair that stick to her face like talons.

'Chloe, please...' I force myself to look into her eyes, her angelic face twisted with rage. 'You don't want to do this.'

A grin comes to her lips. 'I do, Lyra. I really do,' she says, nodding eagerly.

She holds the knife above her head, smiling, and then brings her full weight down onto it. I scream out and twist my body. The blade tears across my palm as I try to fend off the attack. Chloe's breath becomes quicker, more excited the more she slashes at my body. As she leans further in I manage to grab her wrist. A kick in the stomach sends her sprawling backwards and the knife drops from her hand as she hits the cage. Our eyes meet for a second then I quickly scramble over as she scours the dirt. She looks up at me and lets out a sickening wail, the sound penetrating the roar of the storm; 'You made me kill him!'

In an instant she's back on top, straddling me, her sharp nails clawing at my face. 'He's dead because of you.'

I feel myself giving up, curling into a ball and covering my head with my hands.

This is it. This is the moment I die.

Another ear-piercing scream is followed by the sound of rushed voices.

'Hold her down!'

I open my eyes and see Marie yanking Chloe back by her hair. They both topple backwards, Marie now buried beneath Chloe who is bellowing with such a soul-deep hatred that it drowns out the fall of rain. Jackson appears and grabs hold of Chloe, pushing her face into the metal wire of the cage as her arms and legs lash out like a demon. After a few moments Chloe submits, and the flailing stops. Her voice is now no more than a whimper; 'Lyra, help me.' A jumble of sirens distort my senses as flashing lights illuminate her face in staccato bursts of red and blue.

As I nurse my hand my eyes meet with Chloe's one last time. Although my body is in shock, and anger still simmers, I still can't help but feel sympathy for this girl. Her huge, dark- brown eyes glisten, just like the day I walked into the Warren's life just over a week ago, only this time the tears are of deep, deep sadness. I had great hopes of helping Chloe. And like everyone else in her life, I've failed.

Chapter Seventy-Four
Lyra

'Here you are, *Bonita*, a nice cup of English tea, strong and sweet.'

Marie adjusts the knitted blanket she's draped around my shoulders and sits beside me on her worn-out sofa. 'How's the hand and ankle? Do you need more painkillers?'

I lean back against the headrest and gaze at her for a moment. After everything she's been through these last few days, she's still thinking of me.

'I'm grand, but thank you. You ought to get some rest yourself. It's been a crazy twenty-four hours.'

Yesterday's events now seem like a dream, as though they happened to somebody else. I know I'm yet to process everything; not only how about close I came to death, but also over the memory of what really happened the night mammy died and why I have always felt so guilty. 'I turned my back on her and walked away,' I mutter. 'I could have stopped her putting that heroin into her veins.'

Marie rests her head against my shoulder and sighs. 'You know, Lyra, even if you had intervened that night, your mother would have used again. It wasn't your fault and you couldn't have stopped it.'

A huge weight lifts from my shoulders, knowing that Marie is right. Instinctively I turn and kiss the top of her head.

We remain this way for some time, connected in a way I've never experienced before.

'I hope the good Lord will see to it that Chloe gets the help she needs now,' says Marie at last. 'She's a troubled soul.'

I find myself nodding despite the underlying anger that still burns inside of me whenever I think of her. But even after everything she's done, there's still a whole load of pity too. 'I suppose if she's ruled sane though, she'll be going to jail for life for Bill's murder.'

'She will. Though how anybody can say that child is sane, I don't know. I promise you, I've never met anyone quite like her, nor any family quite like the Warrens.' She crosses herself, takes a sip of black tea, then stares off into the distance, the silence between us so comfortable now, as though she's always been with me. I'm certain I must have known her before, loved her before, in another life perhaps.

I guess me coming here did some good after all. Jackson, for sure, was suffering before I arrived and now he can begin to live his life the way he wants to, for himself instead of being shackled to Bill's chains. He's also learned that his mother didn't abandon him but was killed. Gloria too can return home and care for her mother and child, safe in the knowledge that despite her fear, she spoke out and sought justice for Dee.

But I realise that coming here and meeting Marie has also healed me. Marie loves me for who I really am and has shown me how to love myself. In her eyes I see my past, my present, but most importantly my future. I see myself and know, for the first time, that I am enough.

I turn to Marie and wish I could find the words to tell her how much she means to me, and that no matter what the future holds, no matter how many miles we're apart, we'll remain together always.

She places her hand on mine and squeezes tight. 'I know, *mi Bonita*.'

My eyes fill with tears and, finally surrendering to myself, I cry. And you know what? It feels like a smile.

Epilogue
Lyra: 2 YEARS LATER

'Fiction is a lie. Good fiction is the truth inside the Lie.'
Stephen King

I SIGN MY NAME ON THE FLYLEAF AND HAND THE BOOK to its new owner. 'Thanks for buying, I hope you enjoy it.'

'Do you mind? I adored Mother.' The lady puts her face next to mine and pouts at an iPhone. I barely have time to smile before she's uploading it to Instagram with the hashtag #booksigning.

I scan the heads of a long, snaked line of readers; each one having battled the cold Irish drizzle to buy my book, to see me. Waterstones in Cork hasn't been this busy since Graham Norton's A Keeper tour. Even the prospect of hours spent in small talk isn't enough to dampen my mood.

I pick up another shiny hardback from the pile and take a moment to appreciate it. It feels heavy, though not from the weight of its words but from each memory folded between the pages. If Mother was my heart bled dry, then this beauty has pumped that blood back through my veins.

'Hello Lyra.'

The voice makes my stomach churn. 'Jack!' His name rolls off my tongue like a dark secret.

'Or do you mean Jackson?' His neutral tone and expression give nothing away. Typical Jack. 'Hardly gone all out to hide our identity, have you? I ought to sue you.'

'Look. I know I should have asked your permission but...' I stop, relieved to see a smirk pressing against Jack's pursed lips.

'Eyes of Glass.' He runs his finger over the embossed title in his hand. 'Were you referring to my unnaturally green eyes?' he asks, making air quotes. 'Or my stepsisters lack of soul?'

'How is she doing?' I ask, my voice thick with emotion. Despite everything, I still have a strange maternal pull towards Zoe, (or Chloe if you prefer).

'The same,' says Jack, rolling his eyes in the same way he always does when speaking of his stepsister. 'Still trying to pin Delores's death on my dad and still appealing his death on the grounds of abuse. She'll never change.'

Silence stretches out between us as Jack, like me, seemingly reflects on the past.

Using my experience in Chappaquiddick as the basis for my next novel, wasn't an easy decision, yet it occurred to me that the best fiction often derives from truth. Writing Eyes of Glass was both my healing and my truth. Ultimately, it was my story to tell.

'Come on then, are you going to sign it for me?' Jack passes me the book and I scribble my name. I wonder if I ought to add a message, but his presence has triggered writer's block of the worst kind.

'Sorry I've not really been in touch,' I say, passing back the book. 'I needed time to process everything. How've you been?'

'Great.' For the first time ever, I see a smile reflected in his eyes. 'Living with Brad...sorry, Brett to you,' he adds, laughing. 'I'm slowly selling off all dad's estate and then we plan to travel. Who knows, we might stop off in Galway. I've heard the people are pretty cool there.'

'You should. We'd have some craic I tell you.'

'Some what?'

I laugh, realising that some things never change. 'Never mind.'

With the next-in-line now theatrically checking her watch, I wave Jack goodbye and tell him to keep in touch.

'One more thing before I go,' he says. 'Who is Marie? We had tons of housekeepers as you know, but none like her.'

My heart smiles as I remember Marie, the only character who I fabricated, and yet to me she was more alive than all the rest. I may have breathed life into her in the first instance, but it was she who rewrote me, who, through the endless nights of writing, and digging deep into my soul so that the truth may flow through my fingertips, made me realise that I was not to blame for my past. Most importantly, Marie showed me that although mammy may be gone in body, she is still very much alive in my mind and soul.

And that, is the real beauty of fiction.

The End.

We'd love to keep in contact with you and let you know what's happening in our crazy co-author world (life is never dull with Joe and Gemma!), so please leave us your details here and we'll be in touch.

Acknowledgments

First and foremost, thank-you to our families and loved ones, as without your support, *Eyes of Glass* would never have made it out alive... nor us for that matter!

These past two years have been challenging in many ways, but as we write this today, life is good, and we are both exactly where we ought to be. So, to Joy, Tom, Gemma's Mum, Dad and Nanna, and our respective offspring, Molly, Sam, and Jude, we thank you for being our light and our lifelines.

Thank you also to Sumaira and Nikki, for being incredible publishers and the best humans. We've found our tribe in you, and we're so excited to continue this journey with you both.

Big shout out to Tracy Fenton at TBC (The Book Club) for the sensational blog tour, and of course, for all the reviewers who tirelessly support authors like us.

And to the Queen of Thrillers, Angela Marsons, you're inspiring, incredibly talented, and the nicest of people. Your support means the absolute world, matey.

Finally, to all our readers. Without you, we wouldn't have a writing career. Your support means more to us than you will ever know.

Gemma & Joe

Joe, I wind you up daily, but I couldn't have gotten through these last few years without you. I will be forever grateful to you for being there *that* day, and for all the love, help and support you have given to me and Jude since. Anytime, Always, my friend.

Gemma

Gemma, it's been a ride! You've helped me just as much as I've helped you. We're a great team in so many ways, and I know we will both be there for each other, *Anytime, Always.*

Joe

About The Authors

Gemma Metcalfe is a full-time author from Manchester, England. She started on her career path at age five, winning a head-teacher's award for her epic debut novel, *Nan's Tree*. Since then, she's published four books, both in her own name, and with Joe. The duo have also worked together as ghostwriters on many books and screenplays.

Gemma admits to having a rather warped imagination and loves nothing more than blindsiding her readers.

Angela Marsons said of her, 'This author has a very bright future ahead of her', while B A Paris called her first thriller, 'a brilliant debut'.

About The Authors

Joe Cawley is an award-winning author and travel writer. He's lives in the hills of Tenerife with his family and an assortment of other wildlife.

His words have appeared in just about every national newspaper in the UK, including *The Telegraph* and *The Guardian*, as well as the *New York Post*, *Taipei Times* and *Conde Nast Traveller*.

As well as veering to the dark side with Gemma, his trilogy of humorous memoirs, *More Ketchup than Salsa*, was voted 'Best Travel Narrative' by the British Guild of Travel Writers and has sold over 100,000 copies.

Also by The Auhtors

Our Little Lies

Trust Me

A Mother's Sacrifice

Printed in Great Britain
by Amazon

32157583R00148